Stephanie Percival

Published by TriskeleWrites
30 Green Lane
Higher Poynton
Cheshire
SK12 1TJ
 ISBN 978-0-9562958-1-1

British Library Cataloguing in Publication Data. A CIP record for this book can be obtained from the British Library

Designed and typeset in Garamond by TriskeleWrites. Cover design TriskeleWrites from original artwork, 'Winter Oak Tree' by Marilyn Barbone © agency: dreamstime.com

Printed in Great Britain by the MPG Books Group,
Bodmin and King's Lynn

The Memory of Wood

20/01/2011

To,
Chris & Becki,
Hope this encourages you
to visit Northamptonshire.
Love from
Stephanie.

Prologue

Fotheringhay Castle, February 8th 1587

She watched the dawn come. Stretched fingers of light from the small window smudged pale circles onto the dusty floor.

It had arrived.

The day she would die.

Through the windows she could see mist carpeting the frozen February fields. Ground so unyielding it gave her no comfort. Occasionally in its green blandness it cast away her melancholy but today it conspired against her as did her enemies. How she longed for the dramatic crags and skies of Scotland or the gentle sweep and warmth of the French countryside. No, she was to die here in this obscure place that held no consolation of home.

Today from her viewpoint high in the castle tower she could not even glimpse the river, only the crooked willows crouching like praying entities. The dampening mist extinguished any hopes of spring, masking green shoots or searching tendrils. Yesterday she would have sought signs of the spring that would surely come but now the world was without colour, and optimistic thought was slipping from her. Sometimes she felt she was fading, all colour leeching away like blood dispersing into a flood of water. There was no hope.

Her lady-in-waiting laid out the black dress she would wear. It hung over the chair like a dead thing, a carapace cast away. Momentarily she thought of an insect shedding one skin and metamorphosing to another, an ending leading to a new beginning; but the idea was fleeting and left a trail of icy hopelessness. She put the dress on. The buttons were fastened, small shining acorns so cleverly crafted and so difficult to hook together.

She was glad she had completed her writing and contemplation the night before. Her hands would not move now; they seemed incapable even of turning the rosary in her hands. The beads were usually so easily warmed into vibrancy and colour but today just hung limply. The crucifix with its carved figure seemed far from her, His resurrection, which she had been so sure of during the night, had drifted into a mere possibility and her guilt mingled with her fear.

Finally her little dog came to her. She was aware of the warmth of his body in contrast to everything else. However, she could feel him shaking though he couldn't know what the day would bring, and each time she moved he would whine and cower under her skirts.

The knock on the door came. Then descent. Down the tall tower, spiralling around and onto the wider dark staircase. She put out her hand to steady herself and gripped the wooden rail, its strength reassuring for a moment. Then she moved onwards in a trance. She was sensitized to everything so each creak of the floor beneath was like a whip cracking. Besides the thud of her heart beat was another quieter tick as if a clock was counting down time marking the few remaining minutes of life. She was aware of the blackness of the wood. Such dark wood. There are no riches here, nothing shines, she thought. Such wood will surround me forever in the cold ground. She did not even know where she would be laid to rest. Her fear surrounded her like fog. It stained her and seeped from her contaminating the air around her, so it was all she was aware of, as if somehow she did not exist in the physical sense but simply hovered as a bubble of fear. The wretched stench of it permeated everything. The posy of herbs, pressed into her hands by a lady-in-waiting and now swinging from her belt, could not conceal it.

The rosary between her fingers rattled, not in the comforting response of prayers but like the beating of bones.

As she crossed the hall to the stage, the hollow echo of her steps was loud in her ears. The ominous drum call to her fate.

The stage was set.

Now she must die.

Chapter 1

The Talbot Hotel, 2006

It had been one of those evenings. And it was not yet finished.

My resolve had been tested and found wanting and then I had been forced to confront memories that I desperately wanted to avoid.

For the moment, I had taken refuge from the world and wintry weather at the bar of the Talbot Hotel, sitting in what some people thought of as my usual position.

In my pocket was a damp, crunched up ball of paper. When I thought of it, the shadow of failure I imagined as my constant companion seemed to grow.

I had spent part of the early evening hanging around outside a sports hall in a town ten miles away. I had intended to go into the meeting. Somebody, I presumed my ex-wife, had put an Alcoholics Anonymous leaflet through my door, and though I had plucked up the resolve to get to the venue I had been unable to cross the threshold.

But, it was on the bus on the way back that I had been really spooked. The bus was nearly empty; it had an odour of grime and dirt, and an underlying tarring of nicotine which never seemed to disappear even though a smoking ban had been in place for years. It reminded me that I had once been a smoker. I suspected I carried around a similar permanent taint.

As I made my way to the back of the bus I picked up a discarded local newspaper. Its half concealed headline caught my eye. Sitting, I unfolded the paper and read:

'Local Girl Goes Missing.'

'Thirteen year old schoolgirl, Emma, reported missing. Police appeal for information.'

There was an accompanying photo probably one taken on a picnic some time ago. The girl looked very young, sitting with her legs tucked up, her pale thighs white against the red of her shorts.

She resembled my daughter Laura. And I was jolted by the remembrance that Laura was dead. A sharp stab of grief shot through me making my eyes water.

Emma was the same age as Laura had been when she'd had her accident. A sense of doom enveloped me. I shuddered as I thought of another child lost. Tossing the paper back onto an empty seat, I watched rain speckle the windows not wanting to confront the sensation the headline had triggered.

Looking out into the early evening darkness I was unable to see anything but the black shapes of trees and bushes rush by. Inside the bus the strip lights were on, locking us in from the countryside we passed through so I was barred from seeing anything lost in the night. I could only see my reflection travelling with me, appearing to hang in the blackness outside the bus windows, a doppelganger with a distorted frown.

When the bus deposited me in Oundle's market square I had practically run to the Talbot for sanctuary, downing my first pint and a chaser speedily to blur the edges of Laura's death. Now I had drunk enough to dull my thoughts.

The room was quiet and calming, warmed by a crackling fire now burning low. The punters who played the juke box and slot machine had long given up. I knew I would soon be asked to leave but didn't want to think about my lonely walk into the cold, wet night. So I hunched down on my stool trying not to allow my thoughts to wander. Instead I listened to the cracking of the logs on the fire and waited for Mac, the barman, to order me home.

So what he said when he did speak threw me.

"Mary Queen o' Scots is walkin' agin, Phil."

I looked up at him. From my slumped position across the bar counter and in my confusion I thought he had said 'scotch'. I nodded towards the relevant optic, trying to keep the movement minimal to avoid aggravating the ache in my head. Mac filled a tumbler with amber liquid and I anticipated the end of another evening. I sipped the scotch. The taste was pleasantly bitter; my mouth had become dulled from an evening of drinking beer.

Mac and I had spent many evenings in this companionable non-verbal communication particularly on cold, wet nights when most respectable folk were home already. Occasionally they ended with a glass of scotch and a few words about the beautiful liquor and its miraculous transformation from mere water and grain. I guessed it was when Mac was also feeling melancholy and far from home.

Tonight the conversation took another track.

"It's the anniversary of her execution on Wednesday, ye know?" Mac said.

"What?" The sentence penetrated the dull swimming in my brain.

"Mary Queen o' Scots, you know? Her ghost." Mac's burly figure moved around the small area behind the bar. He wiped a pint glass with firm efficiency, moving easily in spite of his size in the confined space.

"Mary Queen of Scots," I mused.

I picked up the glass and admired it for a moment. The contents gleamed, kaleidoscoping capricious crystals of light around the walls as the dwindling firelight played over the cut-glass surface.

"Mary Queen of Scots," I slurred again, liking the sound of the words.

"Well ye know about my ancestor don't you, man? She's supposed to walk the stairs."

I did recall the old story. The ghost that haunted the staircase. Mary Queen of Scots had walked down it on her way to her execution at Fotheringhay, when the stair case was still part of the castle. In the other area of the bar was a painting of her descending the dark, wood steps, with her sombre entourage and the legendary little dog at her heels. Like many castles, Fotheringhay had been taken apart and used in local buildings. The Talbot Hotel, an old coaching inn, had acquired the staircase.

"You don't really believe that stuff, do you?" I asked, knowing it was more usually the sort of comment Mac kept for the few American tourists who strayed to Northamptonshire in the warmer months, searching for links to Princess Diana and Shakespeare and their long lost relatives.

Mac enjoyed winding them up. He'd put on the MacDonald tartan and play the bagpipes and insist he was related to Robbie Burns. Tonight, the bagpipes hung forlornly in their usual position above the bar collecting dust. Mac was certainly proud of his Scottish heritage; I knew he had made the move south as a last resort. I didn't know the whole story just that his younger brother, Jamie, had been under pressure to leave Edinburgh.

I looked at Mac's broad shoulders, noticing the tail of tattoo that escaped his short sleeved shirt and thought he must be taking the piss.

"So you've seen her then?"

"No not seen, but sometimes there's a coldness and the presence of something." His Scottish lilt made the thought more chilling.

"It might," he started and hesitated. Even in my inebriated state I realised there was another agenda. Mac was not adept at lying.

"It might make a good story though," he finished quickly.

So that was his game. He wanted me to get back to writing and drum up some custom for him at the same time.

"Has Sarah put you up to this then?" The turn in the conversation was making me feel a little more sober.

"No, Phil. We just thought," he coughed, so I knew Mac and my ex-wife had been plotting. "I", he stressed, "just thought it was about time you did a bit less drinking and maybe some work would help."

A spark of anger flashed behind my eyes.

"The paper threw me out, remember?" I said with venom. A brief image of my boss shouting at me moved fleetingly through my head.

"But you could freelance, like you do with the photos."

"Well thanks for the thought, mate!" I replied sarcastically, "but I'm not a hopeless case." As I said the words I realised I might not win that particular debate.

I drained the dregs from my glass and thumped it onto the bar.

"What's tha' bout you being a hopeless case, Phil?" said a voice behind me. Jamie, Mac's brother had come into the room. The ceiling seemed lower due to his height. The brothers at first glance appeared quite similar, the same build, but Jamie was a couple of inches taller. They both had cropped red hair and strong features which betrayed a Viking ancestry, but where Mac's mouth was broad with a ready smile, Jamie's seemed thinner, more often in a hard line. You were never quite sure where you were with Jamie. He switched the charm on and off, sometimes you weren't even sure when. So, although Jamie could be quite approachable when he wanted to be, Mac's easy going nature made the comparison harsh.

Jamie walked towards the bar and gave me an overly firm pat on the shoulder as he passed.

"Nice to see tha' old jacket, Phil. Does it crawl out to greet you in the morning?" His lips had curved upwards but I wasn't sure if he was smiling. I bought the green Barbour jacket with my first pay packet, when as a junior reporter I was sent on the worst countryside assignments. We've been through a lot together; it's good to have something companionable to cling to when life is so precarious. I am very touchy about my jacket and felt hurt, though the beer may have added to my sensitivity.

"Well, you're not looking great yourself," I said with the tunnel vision of drunkenness making me pick up on his unusually untidy hair and crooked shirt collar. Jamie shrugged and moved around the bar fiddling with the cash till, his back towards me. The conversation stopped whilst he printed out a stream of till roll. He didn't stay long and I thought he slammed the door on his way out.

"Oops, looks like I've upset him."

Mac said nothing but started to drape towels over the taps and taking a cloth, wiped the bar with unnecessary force. I knew Mac hadn't meant to distress me but I couldn't write. When I tried to sit down and write the only word that flowed from the pen was 'Laura, Laura …' and occasionally 'Why?'

I sat miserably at the bar my head hanging down, memories of Laura churning round and round, as I watched Mac's hand and the cloth moving in steady circles.

"Look, man. I know it's hard for ye but maybe ye need to start living your life again. You were a good journalist."

Mac was trying to be helpful, I knew that, but I didn't really want to live again. That's why I was always in here drinking, living a kind of half-life. Pain had become a symbiotic mate; I did not repel it, so like ivy it continued to creep upon me growing ever thicker, engulfing me in my own misery. Here, at the bar I usually didn't have to think about my daughter's accident. I could imagine she was safely tucked up in bed, Sarah sitting crooked up in the corner of the settee reading and listening to music. If I tried to live in the real world, I'd have to face up to all I had lost. I'd have to admit Laura was dead. I'd have to accept my failed marriage. And acknowledge my family had been torn apart. No, I didn't want to do that. I continued to sit in my miserable pose. My head swung a little as if weighted improperly.

"It's time to go home," Mac said gently.

"Wait!" I shouted the desperation to stay more acute now Laura was fixed so firmly in my thoughts.

"Let me stay a while, see if I can't get the feel for a story. You never know I might be inspired." I smiled pleadingly at Mac, knowing it was a lie as I said the words but it would save me having to go to the grotty flat I now called home, for a while longer.

"Okay. Just a few minutes mind, I want to lock up."

I had lost account of the beer I had poured down my throat during the evening; the alcohol was a heavy, sloshing pool in my head. My steps were a little unsteady as I made my way from the bar up the few steps and through the glass panelled doors into the stairwell. It was a confined area between the old world charm of the public bar and the hotel reception.

The staircase loomed narrowly above me; its heavy square cut timber overwhelmed the restricted space. The dark oak was black in the low lamp light. My vision swam so I held onto the banister glad of its smooth solidity beneath my palm. I stepped up on to the first tread.

There were four steps up to the next stage where the staircase turned. I was aware of my feet in their grubby trainers, incongruous with the rich red carpet.

"How many feet have walked here?" I wondered idly as my heavy legs made their way unsteadily up the next flight.

I was about half way, having reached the first landing that led off to a corridor signed to the Fotheringhay and Mary Queen of Scots suites. I turned and sat on the step and was able to see a little way down, although the central pillar obscured the view into the hall. My position was well lit compared to the hollow blackness below. A waxing moon was temporarily released from scudding clouds. The clear portion of sky was oval around it, creating the impression of a huge eye peering in. Light streamed through large leaded windows opposite me and created acute, shadow lines cutting blackly across the space like dark rods, it enlarged my crouched figure and projected the shadow onto the wall. The illumination mocked me, a constrained monster captured inside a cage.

As I looked across at the black squareness of the banister rail the moonlight blinked so the wood became momentarily mobile. It appeared like a thick tarring of liquid able to catch up the dust and debris of the stairway. In my giddy state the seeming movement fascinated me; I stared at it more keenly, trying to see the knots and grain which should make it solid wood. There were deep furrows and the hint of lines which aged the wood, but they were circular whorls like fingerprints which gave the appearance of eddies in the structure, sucking whirlpools which funnelled my thoughts. I imagined I could feel gravity from them pulling me in. I reached up to touch the rail nearest me. It was surprisingly warm. I thought my hand might leave an impression in it, absorbing my palm print on it. It would remain there as evidence of my presence. One I could not deny.

The cloud cover across the moon continued to break and fuse making the banister ripple in the stroboscope effect. My thoughts continued to go round and round, though now I was sitting the sensation of alcohol in my head was not unpleasant, rather a dizziness which blurred reality. I was not upset at the idea I might be sucked into the molten stream of banister and disappear.

The air was cool and quiet; I could hear the familiar comfortable tick of the grandfather clock drifting up from the empty hall.

Even though I was less than sober I realised I must look pretty foolish sitting here. But in late January the Hotel's guest rooms were hardly in use so it was unlikely I would be observed.

It was now that I really missed smoking, when I was sitting waiting for time to pass. Laura had made me give up. She'd done a project on smoking at school and, indoctrinated with visions of tarred lungs and furred up arteries, she had nagged me, as only a nine year old can, managing to pepper me with unanswerable conundrums until I promised to give up. She'd put a pink piggy bank in my studio and the money I saved went towards her first proper SLR camera.

It transpired she was a natural photographer, able to capture the light to mark a moment in time seemingly without effort. We'd spent hours together taking and printing photographs. She'd always been fascinated to watch the print appear as the developing solution moved over the glossy paper. I could visualise her face clearly, etched like a cameo under the red developing light; she had said nothing but her eyes widened at the miracle emerging.

I considered the chemical reactions involved in photography as a magical occurrence deserving of reverence; Laura instinctively agreed with me. It was only as she'd got older that she had wanted me to start using digital photography. I hated the idea. Digital photography was different. The process seemed cold and insubstantial, in comparison, simply information on a computer chip. Developing a print from scratch was real. The process took time: from first framing a picture, adjusting the settings so the perfect amount of light fell onto the film, the balance of the chemicals and the exposure. Having dishes of solution and an enlarger was true photography. You became an integral part of the process.

We didn't even have a computer like most of Laura's friends. She'd laugh and call me old-fashioned. When I thought back that's when she stopped coming and helping me as often and her camera was left to accumulate dust on the studio shelf.

From the inside pocket of my jacket I retrieved a crumpled photograph.

Laura's bright eyes looked straight at me. It had been taken on her thirteenth birthday. She'd put make up on and had struck what she thought was a grown up pose. She was wearing a soft velvet hat which had been given as a present and the purple colour covered her brown curls, emphasising their shine. As we had developed that photograph, the brilliant colour seeping into the white paper, I'd had the sudden realisation she was no longer my little girl and I wouldn't have her company for much longer. I imagined her spending time with friends, going to college, eventually moving out. Sitting there on the stairs, it hit me like a stomach punch; I had never considered she would be dead.

I stared at her motionless features.

The silly verse about 'Half way up the stairs is the stair where I sit,' came into my head. I silently tried to reassemble the half-forgotten words and tune. Just as my brain could not recreate the song, so, too, Laura had faded in my memory. It was a guilty truth that without the photograph my recall of her face was poor. I could not evoke the elements of her features, only recollect her personality. It was the compacted mush called paper that was able to retain the image of my little girl.

'Half forgotten', 'Half-way', my life had reached a midpoint of stagnation. Everything was distorted and out of focus.

I wondered if I'd dozed off, because the chime of the clock seemed to jolt me. I felt cold, freezing cold, and pulled my jacket's familiar mustiness round me more tightly. There was an irritation in my nose and I was sure I could smell lavender and rosemary. A draught of frozen air chilled the nape of my neck, so I could feel the fine hairs lifting. The current moved the air around me, pressing gently like an invisible balloon pushing past. My head was groggy but I thought I heard the swish of material and the sensation that somebody or something had walked by.

I sat quite still. Was it a ghost moving past, or was it just drunken vapours?

The photograph was still in my tightening grip and a wink of moonlight gave the shiny surface an animated sheen. Laura smiled at me. She was trying to speak to me.

My head felt remarkably clear. Suddenly, like the blossoming of a very rare and long awaited flower an idea struck the poor, tattered nerve endings in my brain. It *was* the ghost of the long dead Queen. Mary Queen of Scots' ghost was imprinted on the ancient timber, I was certain of it. Like a photographic negative somehow her spirit was bound up with the woody composition. And if she was locked in this staircase, then Laura could still be imprinted in the trees and wood near the road where she was killed.

"Phil! What the hell are ye doing? You should have been home hours ago."

Jamie walked up the stairs towards me and pulled me to my feet.

"I think I just….she was here," I rambled, and looked behind me as he helped me to the bottom of the stairs.

"Who?"

"Mary Queen of Scots."

"Come on, old man, ye need sleep. D'ye think ye can get home on yer own?"

I nodded weakly.

I took a last look at the photograph before putting it safely away in my pocket. But as I did so I made a muttered promise.

I wasn't going to write an article, I was going to find her. I could find Laura's ghost and tell her I was sorry.

Chapter 2

I suppose being close to despair and madness occupy similar levels of emotion. I advanced from the orbit of misery to one of elation; some might say, crossing the boundary between sanity and lunacy. I skipped home as if charged with energy from a new source, ignoring the January rain. I bounced along the street in synchronization with the raindrops as they splashed onto the cobbles of the market square.

Even though the security light came on, I fell over the bin at the back of the café yard and was rewarded by a hiss from Ratty. Once she recognised me she came a little closer and followed me up the wet metal steps that led to my flat above the café. She remained behind me, a diminutive shadow in the yellow light.

The skinny cat was a virtual stray. She had taken up squatters rights in the café yard, and since I had moved in I had allowed her, encouraged her if you like, up to my flat. Neither of us admitted it to the other. I didn't try to stroke her nor did she wrap herself around my legs, but we liked each other's company, both being a little short of friends. I had named her Ratty because initially, when I found her scavenging among the boxes and bins in the yard, I had mistaken her for a rodent. She was a scrawny, nondescript brown with a strangely hairless tail.

I fumbled with my keys and we proceeded into the flat, the harsh hallway light making our contrasting, muddy footprints a neat fresco on the beige lino.

I didn't feel like sleeping, I needed to think. I made warm milk on the battered electric ring, the familiar smell of singed food filling the room. Ratty and I both had milk. Ratty finished hers quickly and stared at me as I sat at the table, my chipped mug and bottle of whisky next to my elbow, my head in my hands.

My brain continued its wild whirling. The idea of what I was going to do moved into my mind like a bright dot against the muted background of drunkenness and despair. I closed my eyes and let myself see the dot expand into an image of clarity. Now I was sure Mary Queen of Scots' ghost was resident in the Talbot Hotel, I needed to find a way to improve the quality of the apparition. If I could do that then I could repeat the technique to create a clear image of Laura. I sipped my drink hoping it would act like a lubricant to order my thoughts.

It sent me to sleep.

I was rewarded by the sweetest of dreams that bordered on reality. A summer picnic by the local river. A toddling Laura was gambolling through the green, daisy strewn field. I could smell the buttery sunshine releasing the fragrance of summer grass. Laura was wearing a white summer dress with a yellow sunhat which Sarah had made for her. It made her look like a little flower. I knew I was dreaming as the daisies were huge and vividly coloured. I observed myself lying flat in the grass and lazily stretching out and plucking only the daisies in my reach. They seemed to grey and wilt as I placed them next to Sarah. Sarah patiently stitched them together into chains, her lovely hands delicately weaving the green stems. My dreaming self watched her intently as the pink oval of her thumb nail pressed sharply into each frail green stalk. It was momentarily brutal. A drop of blood dripped from each stem.

I came round from my dream but did not want to lose the image of Laura and Sarah. So I squeezed my eyelids together and hunched up into my folded arms as if I could keep the thoughts from dissipating. Yet I was aware of the increase in the rhythm of my pulse and more regular breathing. I would not be able to deny wakefulness for long.

The dream was so reminiscent of an actual day in time: the picnic, the sunshine and Sarah patiently weaving daisy chains. I could remember her look of concentration so clearly. Her head tilted slightly, so the brim of her sun hat didn't quite protect her cheek from the sun. The sunlight was able to caress her skin. I imagined I could see freckles appearing as the afternoon progressed. Each one punctuated her beauty. I remember being tempted to kiss each warm spot right then and there. Instead, I stretched my arm out lazily and tickled her chin with a daisy. Whether this was illusion or reality I could not quite grasp and it did not matter whilst I kept my eyes closed and my real, cold world at bay. I could imagine it was all true. Sarah would have pretended to ignore me and flapped her hand at me as if she were brushing away an insect. But there was a smile hovering on her lips that she couldn't conceal. Lips I longed to kiss.

My level of consciousness increased, and now I was more certain of my memories I slowly opened my eyes and smiled. We definitely had a day like that because I had a photograph to prove it.

The sun had been dimming as I set the tripod up. We were all garlanded with daisy crowns and bracelets and rings. I'd set the timer and rushed to be in the photograph so the three of us were captured, laughing together. Sarah and Laura had taken off their hats and in their place were wearing garlands of daisies, white stars against the shining darkness of their hair. We made the perfect family. Sarah and I had enclosed Laura on each side holding hands behind her back, and she had grinned with a gappy smile between us.

The photo had taken pride of place on my desk at work. Until Laura died. I couldn't bear to look at it then.

When I'd been fired from my job I'd accidentally smashed the glass of the frame as I threw it into a packing box. The shattering of glass resembled the damage from a bullet point. It had seemed like a belated omen. Clearing my desk had at least given me an excuse to remove the photo, which only served as a reminder of my broken family, and I'd discarded the damaged frame and secreted the photo away with some relief. I couldn't even remember where I'd put it.

Finally, I realised I could no longer ignore Ratty's meow. Slowly I moved to let her out. My joints were locked and aching, my mouth dry and breath stale. And I had the feeling there was something I meant to do. Ratty's mewling became more insistent. As I let her out into the dark morning, the skinny body was gobbled into dull shadow instantly.

I returned to the kitchen for a strong cup of coffee. It was only as I took in the milk mug with its scummed remains and the open bottle of whisky that I was reminded of the revelation of last night and remembered I was supposed to be on a mission.

I drank thick black coffee to help the ache in my head and after a quick wash under the miserable dribble of water that constituted a shower, and a change of clothes, I headed out into the early gloom.

A cold, damp, January Sunday meant I had the streets to myself.

I made my way to my former home some streets away. The street lamps were still on casting an erroneous welcoming glow. The house was terraced with an archway leading between it and the neighbouring one. I could have gone through the side gate but didn't want to frighten Sarah by fumbling with the squeaking gate, so I rang the bell and waited as patiently as I could, unable to stop myself jigging from foot to foot.

Sarah opened the door, fully dressed and with her hands held up in yellow rubber gloves. I was not surprised to see her up and doing house work; I knew she had difficulty sleeping. She did not seem taken aback to see me.

The protective hand wear was the most colourful thing about her. Her willowy frame was clothed in black jeans and shirt concealing her once curvaceous body; her pale skin had a tinge of greyness, as if gradually absorbing the colour of her clothes.

It was hard to remember her in her former life. Before Laura died. Her transformation was so complete. She had been the one to stand out in a crowd, vivacious and happy. Even if she had worn black in those days her individual presence would effect a happy aura not the morbid drabness it now heralded.

"Come through," she said, standing aside to let me pass, her gloves held up as protective shields in front of her. "I suppose you've forgotten the shed key."

It was a frequent occurrence, hence the resigned look on her face.

There was an instant heaviness of musk in the air. It did not quite cover the underlying stench of bleach. As I walked through the short hallway into the kitchen at the back of the house, I set dangling crystals spinning and chimes tinkling as if I had been caught in an elaborate alarm system.

This was Sarah's coping strategy. I had taken the more usual, destructive path of drink and solitude, Sarah had turned to cleaning and Feng Shui.

Neither appeared effective.

In the kitchen the strip light made the white walls and tiles gleam so I immediately felt filthy.

"I'll bring you a coffee down later," Sarah said as if keen to be rid of me. She grabbed the spare key from a drawer, and I took it anyway.

As I left the brightness of the kitchen and was enclosed by the cold mist draping the back garden, I felt as if I had been abandoned. Stepping onto the small area of grass which separated the shed from the house, I felt as if I was wading into deep dark water, aware there was a sudden shelf where I might stumble and plunge down but having no idea where it was. Sarah had been left on the lakeside, surrounded by her clean crystal palace in which she felt safe, and I was cast adrift, heading for my muddy island.

It had been like this since Laura had gone. For a brief time Sarah and I had clung together. But gradually we drifted apart, bobbing flotsam, caught forever in currents of our own guilt and fear, and unable to find our way back to one another even if we wanted to.

Whilst I pottered in the studio I could imagine I was doing something useful. I could keep up the pretence I needed nobody and I preferred to be on my own to work. Once the studio door was closed against the world I did not have to be accountable. I could forget about Sarah and her dark, sad eyes and the lonely place I could not fill.

I preferred to call the shed, 'my studio'. It gave it a gravitas it probably didn't deserve.

From the outside it was nothing more than a large garden shed, constructed of wood panelling. The original dark staining had faded to an anaemic pallor due to weathering and neglect.

Inside I had managed to create two distinct rooms. The contrast was clear between the clean and tidy work and dark room, with its heavy blinds, metallic cabinet and a battered sink. The other area was my sitting and thinking space.

A tatty old arm chair took centre stage; it might once have belonged to Sarah's Dad at their farmhouse. The sponge cushion was trying to escape its fabric cover. Bits of it broke off from time to time, crumbling onto the floor as if weathered by a malevolent disease. Its desiccation accumulated with dust on the floor. Above, there was shelving on the walls with numerous books about photography and journalism, also liberally coated with dust and competing with the cobwebs for space.

On one wall was a cork notice board. Sarah had made it from the corks of numerous wine bottles dispensed of in the early days of our marriage. It was hard to imagine there had ever been a time that we had drunk wine together, laughing because Sarah needed a few more corks for her project. It had been made before we'd had Laura, when the idea of a child was still a contented dream of a potential life perfectly realised. In our semi-drunken state becoming parents, in due course, was a certainty. But it hadn't been easy.

We couldn't conceive at first. The obstacle intensified our need for a child, like a whirlpool creating a circle of vacuity, pulling all our emotions into the one central theme of fertility or lack of it. For months we could think of and discuss nothing else. Together we'd overcome it. Been drawn closer because of it. I thought we would never have to handle anything so difficult again. And when finally Laura had been born, she fulfilled our dreams.

As a young man I hadn't considered being present at the birth of my baby, but by 1990, the year Laura was born, it was the done thing. So I accompanied Sarah to the hospital. I did not know what I was expecting. The ferocity of pain on Sarah's face was extraordinary. How could this most natural process be so grotesquely painful? For hours I remained in astonished calm, doing what I was asked. It was only later, when I first saw the dark head of my daughter fight against her constraining bands and push into the world, that I was overcome with the sudden realisation; I was a father. I was overwhelmed by the uncomplicated notion that we were a family, a condition I had never consciously encountered before. My own familial connections had long ago been broken. Mother had died when I was fourteen years old, after a long illness caused her to waste away. And I considered I had never known my father. Generally, work kept him travelling away from home and when he had been there we argued. He had died before I met Sarah.

Against the white plumpness of hospital pillows, Sarah's dark head bent over the tiny similar being cradled in her arms and I leant over, drawn into the pool of comfort and warmth emanating from them. Laura was the final link between Sarah and me with her genetic symmetry. As I kissed Sarah, the sheer wonder of sealing our complete family engulfed me. I wept.

How different to the hospital room my present surroundings were, I thought, as I looked around me with sudden nausea.

Once, the cork board had been covered with photos of Sarah and Laura, scraps of paper, ideas for articles, addresses for supplies. Now it was bare except for one curled clipping of newsprint. It held on like a rebellious leaf.

I pulled a few books off the shelves shaking the grime from them, and settled myself in the chair. A little while later I heard Sarah call saying she'd left my coffee outside the door. I knew she would never come in here; it was too squalid for her, just like my present premises above the café. I felt no bitterness towards her, after all her cleaning compulsion was just her way of dealing with Laura's death and no worse than my refuge in drink.

Returning to my present conundrum, I asked myself, how could you develop a ghost? I started with the premise that the traumatic event charged the air causing a reaction within the wood. How you developed that process as you did with a reel of film I was not yet sure.

I thumbed through old encyclopaedias of photography and more modern books in which I had scribbled notes. The squiggles and doodles in the margins, made during my student days, were difficult to interpret. I suspected at the time they had made perfect sense. Somewhere at the back of my mind a thought stirred about a technique for photographing ghosts but I couldn't find any reference to it. A student at college, known as 'Weird Wilf', had been into that stuff. He'd have been described as a Goth nowadays, with his long pale features defined with black makeup and a calf-length, black, leather coat. He'd been the type to hang around Peterborough Cathedral after dark taking photographs of supposedly ghostly phenomena. He'd been especially excited when there was a full moon. I'd kept my distance.

My coffee had gone cold and I packed some books up and took the cup and spare key back to the kitchen. As I approached I could smell cooking. I presumed it must be from next door. I didn't know when Sarah had last cooked a meal. As far as I knew she existed on raw vegetables, fruit and seeds. But the aroma of a Sunday roast was definitely coming from the kitchen and as I put my head cautiously round the door, I could see Sarah standing by the cooker, spotless oven gloves replacing her previous Marigolds. The surrounding surfaces were unblemished as if whatever was in the oven had arrived there by a supernatural process. For a horrified moment I thought she might invite me to stay and eat. Part of me would have liked the suggestion but I knew I couldn't stay in the sterile house, scoured of any trace of my former habitation.

"That smells good," I said, whilst thinking of a way to gently refuse her invitation but she just turned and smiled absently at me.

"Thanks," she said, but made no attempt to make me stay, and I felt a drop of disappointment in my stomach, which I dismissed as hunger pangs brought on by the aroma of cooking.

"Oh, could you go and see Dad sometime," Sarah added as an after thought. "Nobody's been for a while."

I made my way from the house, confused. Why on earth was Sarah cooking? The question remained whilst I determined I would make the effort to do as she asked and visit her Dad.

Her father was living in a residential home in the nearby town of Kettering. Sarah found it difficult visiting him. The residence was pleasant and well managed but Sarah found the smell and seeped in grime of years that pervaded the home gave her a panic attack. Occasionally she would drive me over and we'd take Jim out in a wheelchair, but that was a summer jaunt. I knew Sarah loved her father but the barriers grief had erected were impossible for her to over come. Her older sister, Clare, had moved away when she married. Her visits to Kettering had been quite frequent until Laura's death then the stays became shorter and sporadic, only visiting for an occasional brief overnight stop at a Kettering hotel to see her father and meeting Sarah for a cup of coffee in a café. Her three children, who used to accompany her, were left back home in Surrey.

Laura's death had created a black hole; if you were close you were sucked in, if you weren't you were repelled.

I was half way down the street when I saw Mac walking towards me. His big frame was moving in a way I could only describe as jaunty. His happy face reminded me of a school boy who was resisting skipping. I smiled as I walked quickly towards him. I was pleased to see him and about to ask what he was doing in this part of town and suggest we might have a pint together at one of the other establishments. But suddenly I stopped. The overwhelming sickness of a question answered unfavourably left me reeling. Mac was going to see Sarah. It was Mac she was cooking a meal for. The force that overcame me could not have been stronger if I had walked into a door. They were seeing each other. I'd been so wrapped up; it only just occurred to me that every time I had been in the bar recently, Mac had mentioned Sarah. They were obviously spending time together. I felt betrayed, but my feet kept walking towards him, and I could see his friendly smile forming unconcerned I knew he was going to see her. The only two people I considered friends were shutting me out.

The thought of the Sunday roast cooking, the chicken changing from white edged to crisp golden glaze, made me feel ill, its sumptuousness tainted by the knowledge that if Sarah could overcome her compulsive disorder enough to eat a meal with Mac then she may be ready to share deeper intimacies with him.

Mac slowed down as we met on the path as if he wanted to stop and exchange pleasantries. I deliberately kept moving, mumbling that I was 'busy' but unable to distance myself enough not to take in his carefully groomed hair, the crisp white shirt, clean jeans and shiny shoes.

It was good I had other things to occupy my mind during the afternoon. I kept my head in the books and allowed my thoughts to stray as little as possible. Mac's shiny shoes neatly paired at the bottom of the stairs kept creeping on the periphery. I had a few drinks to blur them.

As I flicked through another book, a piece of paper fell out. I bent with trepidation as I realised what it was.

The misplaced daisy photograph.

It had fallen face down.

Slowly I pinched an edge between my fingers and, before turning it over to see the image, braced myself, as if I was waiting for the needle of an injection to pierce my skin.

I turned it upwards. Laura's smile was like a sunbeam, light that could cut through anything, laser bright. I felt the burn of pain as I looked at it, but the sensation wasn't as bad as I had expected. I found myself able to pick the print up and look closely at it.

My family.

Laura looking out smiling at me. This was her doing. A message from beyond, telling me I was on the right track.

It strengthened my resolve. I had to keep going. I was going to find her.

I didn't put the photo on display; I might overdose on its intensity. I tucked it into the inside pocket of my jacket along with the other image. Now we were all there. My family, close to my heart. With that thought to inspire me, I went back to my books.

Gradually one idea for the experiment formed. I would make a developing solution similar to the one used for photography.

In the photography process the developing solution contains an agent which binds with the silver halides of the film reducing them to silver. If I considered the film medium in this case was the wood, then I needed a similar solution to apply to the staircase which would bind with whatever the particles were within it that held the ghost image. As I read late in to the night, my thoughts warmed with whisky, it seemed to make perfect sense. Except for the details.

The whisky bottle and the luminosity of the moon kept me company. The moonlight beamed in unimpeded by the thin curtains. It hung lantern-like with a smudged halo signifying frost in the morning. I suspected Ratty had used its brilliance to go hunting.

Chapter 3

The days moved quietly from January into February. I woke early, dreading the anniversary the month would inevitably bring. The flat was cold and damp. My rooms lacked the furnishings which might help create a sense of warmth. Everything I had, besides my jacket, seemed to have been borrowed or rented.

When I had first moved out I wanted no reminders of Laura. Even the furnishings Sarah wanted me to take were saturated with a family life that no longer existed. I had accepted some bed linen and towels; that was all.

The flat itself was poorly furnished. There were a few battered bits and pieces which had suffered at passing through numerous hands with no personal interest in their care. It did not bother me. I preferred to live in this tatty minimalism; it meant I wasn't associated with anything.

I scrabbled around for change to put in the meter so I could put the bar heater on whilst I dressed.

Looking out over the yard I was able to discern objects etched with a thick layer of frost. Needing to do something which would keep my mind focused on my photography puzzle, I decided I would go out and take some photographs. Anyway, a local woman wanted some display posters for her shop. It was paid work so I hadn't refused it. I slung my camera bag over my shoulder appreciating the familiar weight. I accepted it like a friend.

The lights were on in the café and I could hear the owner, Mr. Morelli, singing in his tuneful Italian contralto. I hoped he would not come out and rant at me in broken English. Occasionally he would stop me in the yard. I did not understand if he accosted me because he had a grievance about something I was doing or if he was simply passing the time of day in an operatic manner. His gesticulations were such that I sometimes needed to step away from him to avoid being hit.

Sometimes his young nephew would be hanging around in the yard, sneaking a cigarette with a mobile phone clamped to his ear. He would never speak to me. If I greeted him he would merely shrug and grunt at me, as if I was of no consequence, his dark brows creasing over his brown eyes in an unfriendly scowl. There was no sign of him or his motorbike this morning.

I walked down the hill, opposing the general flow of pedestrian traffic. If there was a different feeling in the way the schoolchildren walked together, or the extended conversation between the women on the side walk, I didn't notice then. Looking back there was a vague feeling of a collective twittering as if birds were anxious and nature unsettled.

But on that morning nothing appeared out of the ordinary to me. School children in their striped blazers dawdled by, one or two bicycles on the pavement. I didn't mind. Every time I saw a school girl on a bike I felt an ache in my stomach. I wished Laura had stayed safely cycling on the pavement.

Everywhere was frosted, cold and hard, transformed to a steel and aluminium mosaic, exposing the harsh nature of the world. I took the usual street down towards the river, passed the newly built housing, double garages and manicured hedges. It led me down the track beside hulking warehouses stretching the small town of Oundle out to the by-pass. I passed their grey monstrosity and headed towards the cloudy foam of morning light rising above the slate river.

The river bank was edged with scissoring silvery willows. This was where we used to have our summer picnics all those years ago. The earth had hardened as if it had retained all my memories under glass in an inaccessible museum and would store them forever.

The hum of traffic drifted away as I crunched my way over thin ice on the muddy path. Even the morning dog walkers were absent and I was alone.

I passed the side wall of Ashton Mill. It had been through various incarnations, from mill and farm to most recently a dragon-fly museum. Now it was becoming derelict, with boarded up windows and the white paint work on the timber peeling away like diseased skin.

Taking the track into the warmth of the wood the frost began to dissipate into dampness. The odour reminded me of whisky, the sweet intoxication of fermentation. I stood very still and breathed it in. I let its warmth expand my lungs aware of the chill air around me and the sporadic drips of water from the frost thaw. This was a place near the road where Laura had her accident and I breathed more deeply to try and quell the shaking of my fingers. The trees seemed to sigh, as if they were conscious entities that could tell me the things they had witnessed.

At that moment, I had no doubt I would come back to find Laura's ghost. If her spirit was contactable then this was the place. I just needed to time it right, make sure I had the right equation. I patted the grey bark of the chestnut tree beside me as if I was sealing a promise.

Shaking myself from my trance I decided to get to work. The shots I needed were for a local craft shop. Its window display was full of crystals and stones and pieces of driftwood that had moulded themselves into extraordinary natural sculptures.

Marti, the woman who ran the shop, was equally intriguing. She glided about in vivid velvet creations and positioned herself as earth mother to all. Once she had even tried to hug me, telling me I needed to get in touch with my feelings. I had felt smothered. She smelt of ancient things, of promises made, of primeval secrets and unspoken desires. For a woman who could be no more than forty, she had a sage like wisdom that cloaked her. She was one individual I could believe had been reincarnated and carried the knowledge of those past lives with her.

Marti was a good friend to Sarah and I suspected had been cajoled by my ex into saying she would part with money for my photographs. I was again conscious of just what a charity case I was becoming. Still, I shouldn't complain, it was a job.

The idea wasn't as strange as it had first seemed. As I prowled softly through the undergrowth I found rich, mustard moss with water droplets. Perfect round pearls. I adjusted the shutter speed so the moisture sparkled. Decaying winter leaves adrift on the wood floor had been enlivened by the edging of snowy frost that washed them like the foam on waves. Dark ivy leaves trailed over a tree stump, cast in silver by the ice. Then there were the tree trunks themselves, not only the grain of the bark but ornamented with graffiti. A plump carved heart caught my attention, its central motif a smooth gloss crafted into the rough bark. It glowed like amber as if the wood had been carefully stained, paler against the dark crust of bark. Inside were initials. E.S was clear at one end of an arrow but it pointed to an unfinished letter that could have been the upright of many letters.

It reminded me of Valentine's Day. A day I didn't want to remember.

The photograph would certainly work well in Marti's shop window among the stone heart pendants and earthy Valentine novelties but my own heart felt heavy with the thought. The 14th of February was the day Laura had died.

Feeling satisfied with my work, I was just about to return home when I spotted the ideal composition. It was the colour that caught my eye. A bright crimson dot.

At first I thought it was a berry battling the seasonal shadow-light, but on closer inspection I realised it was a bracelet, a simple circlet of bright red shining beads. It was nestled in the cool shadow of an oak tree and the surrounding leaves still had a lacy edging of thick white, glistening against the smudged background. I moved leaves and twigs around creating unique contrasts between nature's decoration and the man-made adornment. I clicked away weighing up the benefits of sepia prints over black and white.

The morning warmed and it was only as the thaw continued and dripped away the last remnants of the pretty frost that I finally decided to depart.

Usually I would have hurried over to the studio to develop my morning's work, but I found myself reluctant to go. There was a fear I might meet Mac coming from the house. I didn't want to see him or Sarah. I decided to go tomorrow when I would be completely alone for the day with Sarah out at work.

The house seemed subdued the following morning as if keeping secrets from me.

I let myself into the garden through the side gate.

As I opened the studio door I felt a rush of expectation as if being welcomed in. Even the spiders seemed to have been ambitiously industrious. I disentangled myself from a particularly sticky web.

Pulling the blinds down, I immersed myself in the pleasant occupation of processing photographs. I allowed myself to become wrapped up in the comfort blanket of familiar tasks and smells. This was where I felt most at home. I knew exactly what to do and in which order. It was a soothing process without interruption or complication. Even Sarah was not around to bring me coffee and make me feel guilty for cluttering up her space.

Hours later the blinds were up and a row of glossy prints were hanging from the line. The bracelet one stood out, I had muted the background to monochrome so that the round red fullness of the beads dazzled against the sharp crystals of the frost.

I had to show somebody. I didn't want to take them to Marti yet and there were only two other people to choose. I didn't want to see either. Not only did I not want to talk to Mac I wasn't sure if he'd know anything about photography. I knew he read my articles in the local press when I'd still been working on the paper. Occasionally he'd mention something I had written, generally in a positive way. Other than that we used to talk with the bar between us. I considered him a friend but he was probably just a good host, treating a needy customer with hospitality. So, I could really only take the photos to Sarah. Even then I considered my final options; Mr.Morelli or Ratty, neither of whom really had the creative flair I required.

Reluctantly, I made my way to the library where Sarah worked. The building was a modern blot amidst the historical architecture of the old market town. Luckily the straggling branches of fast growing bushes were doing a reasonable job of concealing it.

It was warm inside with a few people pottering around the shelves as if they were seeking refuge rather than a good read.

Sarah was behind the desk, sorting through a pile of books. Her glasses were perched at the end of her nose and she looked quite beautiful. Whilst Laura had been alive I'd taken great delight in their similar features. Now it was just another reminder. Laura had gone. Sarah had a slight smile on her lips, relaxing all the taut grief lines around her mouth and eyes. I sensed with horror that the aura of greyness which had surrounded her for so long had been replaced by something resembling happiness. I was going to creep quietly away before she saw me. The thought of speaking to her suddenly became distressing. But I was too late. She looked up and smiled at me.

"Where's the stuff on Mary Queen of Scots?" I asked with false brightness, ignoring the thousand questions I wanted to ask.

"Over there." She pointed and my eyes followed the direction of her finger. "So, Paul talked to you then?" she said, my gaze returning to her face but not making eye contact.

It took me a moment to realise she was referring to Mac. I was speechless as my mind came to grips with Sarah speaking his name. Using his real name. Another bridge between them that excluded me. Sarah and Paul. Paul and Sarah. Sarah and Mac. Mac and Sarah. It thumped like a repeated head butt and made my thoughts swim. Finally I managed to choke out a reply.

"Yes, he did. And I may be interested." I slid the envelope of photos towards her across the desk top. "Have a look at these. They're for Marti."

She slowly opened the pack with her slender fingers, smiling benignly at me as if I was a child who had done something good.

She looked through each, making encouraging murmurs. At the last one she stopped letting the others drop back onto the desk. She held the square of glossy paper up towards the light, squinting at it, and turning it around as if trying to work out which way up it should be.

I was about to reach out and grab it, saying "This way up!" but before I did she blurted out,

"Philip, you know what this is, don't you?" She looked worried.

"It's a bead bracelet against frosted oak leaves…..a masterpiece taken by the well-known local photographer…Philip Lockley." And I flourished an arm wildly, so one of the prints slipped to the floor.

For some reason Sarah leant towards me and whispered, "It's that girl's."

"Which girl's?" I asked becoming increasingly cross, and felt the other library users look across at me.

"The girl that's gone missing!" she hissed. "Haven't you heard the news or seen the local paper?" She walked round the desk to a rack and pulled the local paper out, unfolding it in front of me.

"There!" she said, her voice returning to normal volume. She stabbed her finger on the leading story.

'Local Girl Goes Missing.'

'Thirteen year old schoolgirl, Emma, reported missing. Police appeal for information.'

"Yes, I've seen that," I said crossly, a strange taste filling my mouth. "What about it?" I asked, really wanting to fold the paper up neatly and returning it to its place on the magazine rack where it couldn't affect me by stirring up memories of Laura.

However, Sarah carefully flattened the paper onto the desk and pointed to the accompanying photograph.

"Look at that."

Frowning I looked more closely at the photo. The pale girl in her red shorts on a patterned rug.

I was about to shrug.

"There!" said Sarah more loudly stabbing her finger against the print, becoming agitated by my slowness. Then I saw what she meant. Trust Sarah to observe the details.

On Emma's wrist was a bracelet. A beaded red bracelet. It certainly bore a resemblance to the one in my print, a similarity I did not want to acknowledge.

"There must be more than one of those." My mouth said the words whilst my brain was spinning. Sarah spoke the words I was thinking.

"In a local wood, when a girl's gone missing. The police won't think it's a coincidence."

I could only shake my head. I didn't know what to say.

I would have to tell the police. I would have to take them the photograph. I was trying to find a way back into the remnants of my life and found I had walked into something horrible. A pit of guilt that was too close to Laura.

In my desperation I shirked any duty or involvement. I leant towards Sarah antagonistically, "You're not going to tell them, are you?"

"Of course. I lost my daughter two years ago. She was just thirteen, like Emma. Emma's only missing though. This might be the key to finding her. I'm not going to let anybody else go through the same misery if I can help it."

Her mouth was fixed in a firm line. Sarah would always do the right thing. I felt relieved that I did not have to take responsibility for it.

I left. As I departed I saw her fingers agitating the prints into a perfect square.

Chapter 4

The nagging drip of anxiety that had been with me since I'd read about the missing girl suddenly became a torrent, mixed with fear from a whole community waiting for news. As soon as I stepped from the library I noticed people talking about the only matter that they could think of. Even if people weren't speaking they had an air of unease about them, just as I did. I wondered if from above a weather balloon might notice the change of atmosphere over the town. The stand outside the newsagents had a wired board reiterating the headline in bold black pen. Even if I had wished it, it was too late to hide from the news and it troubled me. Especially by the following evening.

You take an instant dislike to some people, and some people take an instant dislike to you. In this event the feeling was mutual. If we had been dogs we'd be baring our teeth with our hackles raised.

Unfortunately I couldn't fight him, turf him out or avoid the confrontation.

Detective Inspector Russell stood squarely on my doorstep. He wasn't a big man, but I suspected he was one of those who practised posturing in front of the mirror to perfect his look of superiority, judging by his posed stance and tilt of his chin. He had a fixed upward curve of his lips. This expression might have been an attempt at a reassuring smile. If so, it needed some work. I felt threatened.

I had been expecting the police but thought they would have been here in the early morning. Now the light was seeping from the day.

I stood back from the door, pressing myself against the frame as he walked haughtily in seeming to sniff the air. His female colleague followed closely behind.

I took them through to the small kitchen, where there were two rickety chairs by the table. It was covered with opened books and paper with scribbled writing on.

The other room was my bed-sitting room, and I knew I didn't want D. I. Russell casting his expression of distaste over that. But I was too late to pull the door to before the detective had already been able to observe the mess. In the kitchen he hesitated before sitting down scrutinising the chair for debris. He then indicated I should sit leaving his subordinate to stand, hands held behind her back, feet apart; like his bodyguard as if I might attack the boss at any minute.

Within moments D. I. Russell had stamped his mark on the small room, not just by his posturing but by the strong stench of his after shave which seeped into the dim corners of the kitchen like hyena tongues seeking out a carcass.

Russell pulled a plastic envelope out of his blazer with a flourish as if performing a clever magic trick. He placed the photo I had taken of the red bracelet on the table between us, pushing the books out of the way. He did a neat manoeuvre with his manicured fingers so that it faced me.

"Tell me about this, Mr. Lockley."

I looked at the photograph. Yesterday it had looked so vibrant and startling, but with the unpleasant association it had already taken on a dull grimness.

"It's a photograph," I said.

"I know what it is, Mr. Lockley. Did you take it?"

"Yes."

"Where did you take it?" he said peering at me as if over a pair of glasses. I had a flash back to a difficult conversation with my headmaster. I couldn't remember what I had done but I remembered the premonition of endless detentions.

"In the woods on the Ashton road."

"When?"

"Yesterday morning."

"Why?" He continued to bark the questions at me.

"Because it made a nice picture."

He picked the photo up with a sneer of dissent on his face. "If you say so. It's not my line of expertise. Finding criminals and bringing them to justice is what I do, Mr. Lockley. There's a young girl missing. We need to find her, so it would be better for all concerned if you'd co-operate with me." He turned in the chair so it creaked. Placing his elbows on the table he leant towards me so the books between us piled up on my side.

"Now tell me about the photograph, Mr. Lockley."

I didn't cower from his gaze, but I realised there was no point making an already uncomfortable situation worse, so I answered him.

I told him why I had been in the woods, about the job for Marti's display, and that I had thought the composition had made a good picture for its purpose. I told him, until my ex-wife mentioned it, I had not associated it with the girl who had disappeared, not realising the bracelet was like the one she had worn.

"Other than this bracelet, did you see anything unusual in the woods?"

"No." I shook my head, thinking I was probably not the best person to ask.

"We've been searching the area and found other evidence that makes Emma's disappearance suspicious. Do you know the girl, Mr. Lockley?"

"No, don't think so."

"What about your family?"

I eyed him suspiciously.

"What about them?"

"Do they know her?"

"You'd have to ask Sarah, and my daughter is dead."

He waited, as if he had perfected the timing of his questions to cause his interviewee the maximum amount of unease.

"She died two years ago, is that right?"

"Yes," I said warily, feeling anger rising.

"So she might have known this girl from school?"

"Perhaps," I said shrugging. "Laura would have been fifteen now, so it's unlikely they would have known each other well."

Russell nodded at me as if finally we agreed on something.

"How did she die?" he asked quickly.

I felt off my guard and blurted out, "She was knocked off her bicycle by a car. It was a February afternoon, getting dark, and apparently she swerved out into the road, the driver didn't see her, he had no way of stopping." I excused the driver. I did not mention the faulty rear light on Laura's bike. The faulty light I had failed to mend.

"Where did this happen?"

"Off the Ashton road."

He nodded slowly and brought his fingers together in a pyramid.

"So a similar area to where you found the bracelet?"

"I suppose so," I said, still unsure of the point he was making.

"Our searchers have been very thorough."

I watched him and knew he was scrutinising every movement or reaction I made.

"We found something that might interest you."

He hesitated, keeping his eyes on me. Then slowly he brought another slim envelope from his pocket. Through the plastic film I could see a black band with a clip. It looked like a strap.

I said and did nothing, fearful I might make a wrong move. Finally he continued.

"It's a broken bicycle helmet strap. Obviously been in the undergrowth for some time. Do you recognise it?"

"They're all the same aren't they?"

"No. This one's from a particular make. Your daughter wore a helmet didn't she?"

"Yes. Laura did," I said, annoyed Laura was just another daughter to him. "They said the strap had broken on impact so the helmet had flown off before she landed."

I tried to picture the scene as it had been told to me and had to fight against the horrible image I had conjured.

"We believe this strap is from your daughter's helmet. It was found some way from the site of the accident. We think it might have been broken before she got on her bike."

"Why? And why would she have rushed off if her helmet was broken? She was a sensible girl."

"But she could have needed to escape something or somebody, couldn't she?"

"What...What are you saying?"

Aside from the broken rear light, it had never occurred to me that Laura's death had been anything other than a terrible accident. In that moment, I could feel my forehead furrowing and compressing my brain below into jumbled thought. Was this detective really suggesting something else? As I listened I realised he was.

"I'm suggesting, Mr. Lockley, that your daughter had gone to meet somebody in the wood. Somebody she thought she knew. When she got there it wasn't who she was expecting. Perhaps this person became rough, perhaps this stranger attacked her. Her helmet may have been broken in a struggle. She would have rushed away in a panic, not checking the road as she rode away."

I was speechless; this was a completely different scenario to the one I had imagined.

"Maybe you know all this though?"

My mouth became completely dry and I could not have spoken if I had wanted to. Was he really suggesting I had been involved in Laura's death?

The detective slowly pushed the chair back and got up. His stare didn't leave my face.

"It would be beneficial for us to have a DNA sample, to eliminate you from our enquiries."

Even as he said it and the police officer got a tube out, even as I felt the cotton swab pull against the inside of my cheek, I knew it was not the whole reason for him wanting it. If I refused it would have looked as if I had something to hide. I realised I could not win. It was like playing a grand master at chess. For some reason he had the information or insight to link two apparently unrelated deaths, and I had become an unwilling player in his game. But as I watched him, his smooth complexion masking his intentions, I was sure there must be another motive.

"We've got some more enquiries to do and then we might need to talk to you again, Mr. Lockley. Don't go anywhere."

He said it in a smooth, pleasant way, as if it was merely a polite request, but the words sent a chill through me.

Chapter 5

I had too many things to think about. I needed a drink but didn't really want to see Mac. I wanted to get out of the flat too. Russell's aftershave stained the air, a reminder I did not need.

Some of the questions the detective had asked troubled me. Not the direct questions. They had a yes or no answer. It was those suggestions that trawled somewhere deeper agitating the past so that it could not be ignored.

One of those was the insinuation that if Laura had been a sensible girl, obedient enough to wear her bicycle helmet, then what was she doing in the woods on a dark February afternoon, having told nobody where she was heading.

Why was she there? At the time we had posed the question and accepted the simple answer. She and her friend Kelly had cycled to Ashton Wood after school. Kelly had left early leaving Laura to make her own way home. The fact was they were teenagers who had just been on a school girl jaunt. In our numbed state, we'd believed the story without further delving. But now, however hard I tried, the question would not leave my thoughts. For two years any further enquiry had been suppressed. Now it had returned to haunt me.

I had forgiven the stranger who had driven his car into Laura. I could remember his white face and shaking hands from the inquest into her death. Briefly I wondered what he was doing now. He had seemed distraught; it had not been hard to forgive him. It was simpler to blame myself. If I had fixed the rear light she would have been seen in time. She would have lived.

Laura had remained the innocent party. I had taken the blame for putting her in danger by allowing her out with a broken bicycle lamp. Now I had a nagging feeling that somehow she might have put herself in danger. Fathers protected their children but I could no longer safeguard the memory of Laura's innocence.

There was a sudden noise in the yard. The rev of a motorbike engine and shouts. I went through to the bedroom and peered out into the night to see what the disturbance was. The glowing illumination of the security light presented a group of about six teenagers, boys and girls, louching about. Most had a can or bottle of drink in their hand; some were smoking. In the centre I could see Morelli's nephew strutting. He was a little taller than the rest and probably a couple of years older. His presence in the central intensity of the pool of light looked as if he was performing a play as the main character. The rest of the group circled round him like a devoted audience. He was a good looking and had a quality about him, the way his body moved, the way his mouth talked that drew you to him in the way some movie stars did. A sensation like loneliness hung around me as I looked down at them. But it differed from the feeling of isolation I was accustomed to and I realised I was not envious of the group's camaraderie but jealous of the young Morelli as the centre of attention, a condition I had never experienced.

I watched them for a while longer, the easy movements and laughter, the way each individual moved around but always keeping Morelli's nephew in the spot-light. The voices floated upward, shouts peppered with crudity, the laughter ascending and dispersing like the transitory bubbles of their alcopops.

Gradually I became aware of my crouched voyeurism and was disgusted by it.

I decided that I definitely did need a drink. I would go to the pub and take my chance with Mac.

I slunk down the metal stairs and out through the yard keeping to the shadows. The young group did not seem to notice me at all.

Creeping into the Talbot I was pleased for once to see Jamie behind the bar. I climbed on a barstool and ordered my beer.

"Ye got home alright the other night then, Phil?"

I nodded.

"Bet yer head was a bit sore come the morning."

I nodded again and smiled briefly.

"So where's Mac tonight?" I asked,

"Out courtin'!" Jamie grinned as he placed a pint in front of me.

I wish I hadn't asked and wondered if Jamie had any idea who Mac was seeing.

I huddled in the corner of the bar and sat nursing my pint.

There were a couple of regulars at the bar. Their mumbled conversation seemed to be about the missing girl. It was not the sort of banter usually tossed around here but Jamie, as if drawn into a convoluted game of Chinese whispers, came over and said to me,

"Awful about this missing lass."

"Yes." As I was feeling hung up about my recent interview I added, "I had the police around."

"Nay, no kidding?" said Jamie his eyes wide.

I gave him a run down on my less than pleasant interview with D. I. Russell and Jamie commiserated with me.

"When the filth git on ye back for something, they won't stop 'til they make it stick."

I knew he had been in trouble with the law back in Edinburgh, but the venom of his retort surprised me. If he had been on my side of the bar I'm sure he would have spat in contempt.

He turned and served a customer, but came back quickly.

"Why did they want to talk to ye?"

"I'd found a bracelet, like the missing girl wore. It was in Ashton Wood where I was taking photographs."

"So they believe you're involved?"

"I just took a damn photograph and then they started to ask questions about Laura."

Jamie raised his eyebrows as if in shock. I continued, "I don't know why they think I might have anything to do with that girl or why they should bring up Laura's death, as if it hadn't been an accident."

"So they don't think it was an accident?"

That's what was worrying me, gnawing away since their visit. I continued to voice my anxious questions. "But why would someone want to hurt Laura. Why would the police think that I might have hurt Laura?"

The image of the broken bicycle light came into my head. They could have arrested me for not repairing that. I would have pleaded guilty. But to have harmed her deliberately or abducted another girl was crazy.

"She was a lovely wee lassie." Jamie, for once, appeared to be sympathetic. "And bonnie too."

"Yes. She was lovely."

Too lovely, and too young to have been cut down either by a wayward car or by a malicious act.

Jamie shrugged and was about to say something but at that moment Mac walked in, cheery as usual. He grinned as he lifted the entrance to the bar.

"Aw right, my friend!" he said happily.

I ignored him, unable to face his cheery demeanour, and gazed intently at the surface of my beer, the winking froth vanishing from its surface. After a while I looked up and observed the brothers shoulder to shoulder muttering genially to each other. Comfortable in their space behind the bar. Contented participants in their role of hosts, with the gleam of light and colourful bottles which resembled a stage dressing room with its mirrored backing.

Brothers. I would have liked a brother, particularly a brother, but a sister would have done. With a sibling sharing the load my lonesome childhood would have been easier. If I had a sibling I might still feel as if there was a fragment of family left, like a shard of a priceless broken vase. I envied Mac and Jamie their kinship. There was an age gap of a few years but they had each other. History had blessed them with a familial intimacy which was unbreakable. It was true, blood was thicker than beer. I was always going to be the punter, sitting behind the bar unable to access the brotherly camaraderie which surrounded them. They would always have each other. I was alone.

I felt a wave of beery, self-pitying sickness bubble in my stomach. I was caught like a fish wiggling on a hook. If I struggled against Mac and his relationship with Sarah, I would be the one to suffer. I could quarrel with him but it wouldn't make a difference, he would win. He would still have Sarah, his Hotel and his brother. It might make me feel better but I would end up more isolated, left to drink alone in my flat.

Knowing I was comprehensively beaten, as if to inflict the greatest possible pain on myself, I asked Mac, "You had a nice evening then?"

"The best!" he replied, and I shrunk back a little. It wounded but it would be more beneficial to slip back into this barroom banter. I was up to pretending the thought of Mac and Sarah together didn't hurt me. The strong wood of the bar counter acted as my shield, it prevented me from entering the intimate circle behind it but also it conferred some protection. I needed a similar construction around my heart.

I soothed myself with the thought that at least Sarah was with Mac, somebody I knew and liked. I could keep an eye on him.

"Sarah told me you were looking up Mary Queen of Scots."

"Yeah," and an encore of the Sarah and Mac refrain sounded achingly in my brain.

"Tha's great man."

I'd just have to change the subject. Not wanting to converse with Mac on anything that might involve Sarah, I thought I'd try and find out more about the ghost haunting his staircase. That would be my motivation. I was going to find Laura, I'd let the Sarah and Mac thing be for now.

I motioned to Mac, he poured me a scotch, then I encouraged him to expand on the sightings that had previously been documented as if I was interviewing him to research an article. He seemed pleased to be helping me. I tried to remain the distant professional.

Only a few people had claimed to see an actual apparition of Mary Queen of Scots. Mostly it was feeling a presence, an icy chill in the atmosphere as if somebody had passed them on the stairs.

Usually the sightings had been in winter time, when the weather was wet. Mac had not heard of anyone seeing visions except at night.

"This is just the tales tha' folk have told me," Mac explained a little sheepishly, but he appeared to be quite knowledgeable about it and I reckoned he had been doing some research himself. He remembered one lady guest who had come into the bar screaming, her hair sticking up. She had been heading up the stairs to her room from the hotel reception and seen the vision so clearly she had actually greeted the ghost with a polite, "Good evening."

"I remember it, because we had such a storm later tha' night, it was as if the air was crackling with electricity."

Jamie leaned over and intervened, "Ye've bin watching too many horror films brother. Most times she's seen is when folk have had a wee bit much to drink."

"So you don't believe it?"

Jamie shook his head as if both of us were mad. "Once folk are dead, they stay…. dead."

The bar was nearly empty; Jamie said he'd leave us to our old wives tales.

I returned to my slumped position, my elbows resting on the bar, my eyes following the grain in the shiny wood top as if it was a map that might lead me to a solution.

"Wha' d'ye think then?" Mac said after a time. I wasn't sure if we were still on the same subject or if we were talking about Sarah. I didn't want to talk about her so I told him my theory.

"If a chemical change occurs when light shines onto the film used in photography, then what if a similar reaction occurs in wood when a traumatic event happens; the trauma triggers something within the wood? What if there's a developer that could increase it, a bit like a damp winter night, or the electrical charge in the air when a storm's coming? If I can work out the right formula I'm sure that I could produce a clear image of her ghost. That's what I'm planning."

Mac scratched his head and looked worried. "Philip, when I said ye might write an article I didn't think….." He paused. "Well, this is not wha' I had in mind."

I nearly retorted that when I'd told him I was concerned about Sarah that I did not intend for them to become a couple, but I bit it back.

I just shrugged.

Mac continued to look at me with a worried frown.

"You were the one who suggested investigating," I accused him. The frown deepened. "So you think it's a mad idea?"

Mac still said nothing, but his expression and whole posture were enough to tell me it was.

I climbed off the stool and turned to go, looking back just to say, "Well, mad or not I'll be here on the eighth. The anniversary of her death. I'll be ready by then."

I had only walked a little way outside when I heard heavy footsteps and Mac's voice calling, "Philip, stay a while. Don't go off in a lather."

I kept walking faster until the footsteps behind me stopped.

Chapter 6

I awoke the next morning aware things were changed. In the market square across from the kitchen window I could see the white hulk of a police unit taking up the few parking places. Everywhere I went there seemed to be police officers or a police car. It could have made me paranoid, but rationally I thought they were simply trying to find the missing girl.

A police officer was handing out leaflets to ask for assistance with a police search down by the river and fields close to Ashton Wood. I ignored the proffered paper. D. I. Russell had made it clear that my photograph of the broken bracelet made it more likely that Emma's disappearance was suspicious. Part of me wanted to go and help. However I didn't want to be the one to find anything else in case it implicated me further.

Posters of Emma had been pasted around the town. They had used a more recent school photograph of her. She would not be a child who would stand out in a crowd. A shy face framed by pale hair scraped into a pony tail. Her eyes were large, pale and bewildered. The face appeared uncomfortable at being so prominently displayed; her expression seemed to say 'Why have you done this to me?'

I could feel those eyes watching me as later I walked through the streets.

The whole town was gripped by the news about Emma's disappearance. And like the first spot of a disease it seemed to have triggered a response from the whole country. Her parents had appeared on television, pale and grey faced, sobbing for anyone who knew of her whereabouts to contact the police. I found it difficult to watch their pain spread across newspaper headlines and media sound bites.

I tried not to remember the day I had heard of Laura's accident, but the image was always there, hovering about like a ghoulish shadow. The words, "Your daughter is dead," clanging like a bell. The sky had seemed to evaporate, open up as if the world was being sucked out in an explosion of silence, carrying away everything that mattered, and the unbelievable words echoed in the vacuum and remained like radioactive fall out. I hadn't been able to breathe. What was worse was seeing Sarah collapse as if a neglectful puppeteer had abandoned her. She became wilted. One moment she was vivacious Sarah answering the door, the next she was a hollowed out manikin of her former self. And I could do nothing to save her.

Emma's disappearance brought the horrible sensation back of my powerlessness in the predicaments that life threw.

I went walking to clear my head. There was a police car parked in the market square and once or twice I'm sure I saw D. I. Russell's stocky figure pacing around. I laughed grimly to myself as I imagined him with a deer stalker and magnifying glass searching for clues. The funny picture did nothing to dispel the horror of the situation.

My walk did not help my frame of mind either. Everything was grey, the sky, the street, the shop fronts. February and the dreadful events had drained the warmth out of the honey-coloured bricks that drew the tourists to the picturesque town.

My spontaneous steps took me on a circuit passed Sarah's house, up by the grandeur of the old school buildings and along by the sports field. Two colourful teams were running about playing football making a feeble attempt at dispelling the gloom. Closer up they were muddied, the colour all but extinguished. It was as if the day would not allow any glimmer of brightness. Anonymous young children, watched over by yelling parents, were enjoying their Saturday exercise and competition. The sudden blast of so much life lowered my mood further, but I found myself watching the figures through the iron railings, remote from their carefree play.

As the whistle blew for half-time and the figures huddled into groups I moved away. I tried not to think about Laura joining in childhood games, playing in the park, always screaming to be pushed higher and higher on the swings, until I frightened myself she would fall and had to grab at the swing, at which she would complain, 'Aww, Daaad, don't be such a wuss,' as if I was the child too high on a swing.

Laura, Laura. Her name filled my head. When I remembered her I only had those short thirteen years. Her friends were all growing up, they left Laura behind, forever a child, as they stepped on and into adulthood. I didn't know much about Laura's friends. I remembered pale sweet faces, long hair and pony tails, tears at her funeral. Perhaps they would know more about my thirteen year old daughter who I seemed to have lost touch with in the last days of her life. Perhaps somebody might know what she was doing in Ashton Wood. It was another path back to Laura.

The street eventually brought me out near the library and rashly I decided to go in. I needed to get some books out on force fields. Mac's information about the clearest sighting occurring when the air had been filled with electricity before a storm made me consider using a weak force field as part of the experiment. My general knowledge on such things was limited.

Sarah was dealing with a customer so I quietly went to the Science section and flicked through a selection of books. I found a school physics book which must have been quite old. Its pages were thick with damp and grime as if they had been fingered and thumbed for decades. That was the thing about library books, they told stories of their own. The speckles of dirt and debris, the scent of smoke and sweat. They passed through other people's lives absorbing a trail of intellectual soiling, much as my old jacket took on elements of me and the traces of where I had been. I held onto the musty book whilst I looked at the local history section for information on Mary Queen of Scots. I leafed through a couple of books, my attention not fully on them. I wanted to ask Sarah something and was waiting until the library was less busy. After a few minutes I could see that the other library users were either occupied at the computers or looking for books. Sarah was undisturbed.

I approached the desk, pushing the books out in front of me as a kind of barrier. I looked at her contented face and knew I was going to upset her. She took the books from me and I rummaged for my library card buried in the depths of my jacket pocket. The process was straightforward as she put the card in the reader and stamped the books. I wished the next part of the conversation could be as simple.

"Sarah, do you ever wonder why Laura was down in the woods when it was dark and getting late. Did she tell you?"

I had caught her off guard completely, and her face which had recently become so placid folded itself up into a pinched frown.

"What?"

"I've been thinking about this lately. And I can't work out why Laura was in those woods. It was cold and getting dark and she had no business being there."

Sarah took a few moments to answer.

"What is this Philip? Can't you let it go and move on? She was there. She died. Isn't that final enough for you?"

Our voices were becoming louder in the library quiet. I could sense a lady hovering nearby, wondering whether to come to the desk or not.

"Please go, Philip. This is not the time to talk."

I decided to stay. Picking up the books I made my way to a chair in the corner and waited. Occasionally I felt Sarah looking over at me. I could sense her furrowed brow and dismayed look. I kept reading.

Later I wandered to the magazine rack and collected the local paper. Emma Sutton's story had now been demoted to the third page. Still the same childish photo stared up at me. The image had been reduced in size but was still the only coloured square amidst the black and white print. The bracelet seemed huge against her wrist, great dollops of beaded blood, garish against the paleness of her skin.

Below the article about Emma was another article and two other photographs. One recent one showed the haughty stare of D. I. Russell; beside it the heading:

"LOCAL LAD IN CHARGE".

The second photograph was a grainy black and white shot of a boy in school uniform. It was poorly contrasted so that the grey specks made the image muted. I had to read the small print to realise this was a photograph of a 10 year old D. I. Russell outside the local primary school. I do not think he would have been very pleased.

It did not flatter him. He had been rather a tubby child with a mop of light coloured hair which curled girlishly around the chubby face. He did not look very happy either. His mouth pouting, his eyes black specks scowling. The photos of the children, Emma and young Russell, on the page bore a certain resemblance. The two of them, although separated by time and gender, were victims. The girl came across as vulnerable as if the camera intrusion was unwelcome, whilst the boy looked to be a target for bullies with a soft pasty complexion which would bruise easily. The picture of the surly child who had grown up to become D. I. Russell did not surprise me. Though his expression in the adult shot could not be described as surly there was a hard faced arrogance about it. What was more unexpected, and the reason for the article no doubt, was the fact that D.I. Russell had been born and brought up in Oundle. He had gone to the local junior school but his family had suddenly moved to Peterborough. The article was not clear on the facts and although the words did not say anything, I could tell there was more to the defection than was mentioned; perhaps it was the photograph. Here was a boy who would want revenge for those unknown acts that had occurred twenty odd years ago and driven him from his home town. The face that scowled at me belonged to a person I suspected had returned with scores to settle. Somehow I had got caught up in the retribution.

The time passed quickly. I had actually found out a few useful ideas which I might be able to utilise for the experiment.

I was aware of people coming and going. As the daylight faded and the lights came on there were little flurries of activity. The rain had started; people would come in shaking umbrellas and brushing rain from their clothing. Sometimes the library became quite busy with the automatic doors sucking open and then swooshing closed. I expected it was a background noise you got used to. Gradually though the doors became silent and I was aware the library space was empty.

Finally Sarah called over, "It's time to go."

She sounded reluctant with her information as if she would have rather left me there, locked up in the library overnight. She muttered about having to make sure everything was secured and set the alarm, so I waited for her out side. The early dusk was imminent, the air moist with dropless precipitation.

Sarah fell into step beside me with a sigh and tightened the belt of her raincoat.

"Philip. I know this girl's disappearance has unsettled everybody, but it hasn't got anything to do with Laura."

"That's not what the police think."

"Oh," she said, surprised.

So I filled her in about my chat with D.I. Russell, after she presumably had informed them about the photo with the bracelet.

"So you see, now I'm a suspect, not only in Emma's disappearance but in having something to do with Laura's accident!"

"I'm sorry," is all she said.

We remained silent until we got to her front door.

"You'd better come in," she said as if she had resigned herself to it. "But take off your shoes and that jacket," she added firmly as she opened the door, and then said a quieter, belated, "Please."

We went into the kitchen. I was careful not to touch anything, and perched on the edge of a kitchen chair. I noticed a hole in my sock. The big toe nail, slightly yellow and too long, poked obtrusively out. Sarah would probably notice when she turned round from the sink and it would upset her. I tucked my feet back under the chair so my perched position became precarious.

Sarah calmly filled the kettle and got mugs and teabags from a cupboard on the wall.

"I don't know why Laura was there," she said suddenly, still facing the cupboard away from me as if she might be having a conversation with somebody else. "Of course I've wondered why she was there, but in the end it doesn't really matter. She died."

The force of those two words left a palpable silence hovering in the whiteness of the room. She turned, dragging herself round to face me. When she started to speak again it sounded like gun fire.

"But it was Valentine's Day. For the last few days I knew she'd been arranging something. She and Kelly spent ages in her room. Giggling and secretive. I did manage to sneak in to find out what they were doing. And they definitely were writing Valentine's cards. I thought it was completely innocent. She was thirteen. She wanted to be independent. She wanted to be in love. Girls of thirteen do things like that."

It took me a moment to respond to the onslaught.

"Do they?" I was confused.

"Yes, Philip they do." She crossed her arms sternly in front of her. "Laura was still a little girl to you wasn't she? Somebody to play with once a week when you'd let her come and help you with photography for a treat. She was growing up for goodness sake! You just did the nice bits. You joked with her. I did the clearing up after her. I did the tending when she was sick. I nagged her about homework. I argued with her!" She threw the remarks at me as if she was throwing stones, each one causing painful ripples.

Shaking my head caused the chair to squeak below me. The sound resonated with the bewilderment I felt by the barrage that Sarah had lashed at me. I wondered why I hadn't heard any of this before, painful words hurled from the sack of guilt that bowed us down. Or perhaps I had never listened to the accusations I now realised as the truth.

It was some time before I spoke. Sarah was gulping with an anguish she couldn't seem to expel.

And I was numbed by the veracity of what had been said.

Finally, I was able to speak.

"I wasn't such a bad father, was I?"

Sarah didn't reply immediately, and I couldn't see her expression. Unable to face her I glanced downwards and was again aware of my inadequate hosiery.

"No, you weren't," she answered more quietly, "and I've often asked myself if I was a bad mother, allowing my child to wander off on a Wednesday evening like that because I was too busy with my own life."

"No, you were a good mother," I soothed. I lifted my head and I put out a hand towards her. I had to stand up so the chair wouldn't tip over.

Sarah recoiled and stood upright against the kitchen counter. Forcefully she continued,

"Recently though I've forgiven myself."

I instantly thought of Mac absolving her. I saw his hands reaching out to comfort her and Sarah accepting his touch.

"I think you should forgive yourself too."

Possibly, if we'd had this conversation last week I might have agreed with her, but now it wasn't just about forgiveness, it was about coming to terms with the new portrayal of Laura's accident and finding out the truth.

"I can't. Not until this is finished. You got me into this. Telling the police about the photograph."

I knew I was unfair to blame her for my obsession. We were both just jetsam thrown into a treacherous place, but it made me feel more in control of the situation. That was how blame worked. It was like sharing a problem with a friend. Blame did not really halve the torment but it spread the load so you weren't alone.

Even to my own ears my demands sounded unreasonable. But I continued none the less. "Help me now. I need to know the names of anybody that might know something. What about this Kelly girl or her other friends?"

Sarah shook her head, not because she was refusing to help me, but at my inability to stop the momentum of my compulsion.

She went out briefly and I heard a drawer open and shut and then she returned with a small address book. I could see there were tears in her eyes.

"There are a couple of names here. I think Kelly was really her best friend," she said, sniffing softly. Her shoulders shuddered slightly and I wanted to hold her and let her cry and tell her everything would be alright. Except I knew she didn't want me to touch her and that I could do nothing to make it right. So I let her continue, to struggle on with shaky words. "Kelly Johnson. I think she still lives at the same address. But Laura was friendly with Nicola Osborne just down the road. I know they still live there, I see Nicola pass by occasionally."

As she wrote the names and addresses down in her neat handwriting, still fighting tears and concentrating on keeping her hand from shaking, I tried to recollect these girls who lingered on the periphery of my vision as they had when Laura was alive. I thought Nicola was tall and skinny with braces on her prominent teeth. She had been chatty and pleasant. Kelly I had more difficulty remembering. She must have been the mousy little girl who occasionally came to tea with Laura and said virtually nothing to me; I had kept out of the way only popping in to make a joke or some silly comment that would make them giggle.

I took the piece of paper and stood up to fold it into my jeans pocket. Then I went out collecting my jacket and pushing on my shoes. As I left I could hear the sound of the mugs being replaced in the cupboard.

As it was nearby, I decided to make straight for Nicola's house. My momentum was such I had given no thought as to what I would say as I rang the bell. I didn't wait long before the door was opened by a tall elegant teenager whom I took to be Nicola's older sister. Then, I did a double take. No this was Nicola, grown into a young woman as lovely and self-assured as Laura should have become. Nicola obviously had the same difficulty placing me because she asked a quizzical, "Yes?"

That's when I noticed the braces had been removed and had been very successful. She now had a beautiful mouth I couldn't help staring at.

It seemed incredible that a once gangly girl could metamorphose into such a poised young woman in a mere two years. The change was incredible. I had a sudden longing to see Laura as a woman. From girlish gawkiness and sulking to the friendly, competent woman I supposed she would have become.

"Can I help?" Nicola asked a little more firmly, bringing me out of my trance. Her slender fingers tightened against the door and I presumed she was thinking about whether to close the door on this staring stranger on the doorstep.

"Sorry," I mumbled. "Are you Nicola?"

She nodded very slowly, still eyeing me with suspicion.

"I was Laura's Dad, Laura Lockley. I'm trying to find some information out."

A call came from inside, "Who is it?"

"It's O.K. Mum," she called back and then turned to me, "What sort of information?"

"About friends, boyfriends, was she thinking of running away?"

Nicola squinted in thought and leant against the door frame. I'm not certain how aware she was of the seductive pose it made.

"She didn't have a boyfriend that I know of but we did all like to go to Morelli's café after school and drink coffee and talk. Boys used to chat us up." She said it in a haughty way tossing her long blonde hair off her shoulder as if she had long since passed that phase.

"I don't think she'd be the type to run away but I don't know really. We didn't hang out much that year; she was more friends with Kelly. Me and Kelly didn't really get on." She continued with easy candour. "Kelly was one of those types who only wanted a best friend and wouldn't really let Laura hang out with anybody else. Maybe Kelly would know more."

She shrugged, again making me uncomfortably aware of her developing body. I thought I'd better leave.

"Well, I'll try and see Kelly. Thanks for your help." I turned and walked away aware of her lounging on the doorstep watching me go.

Nicola hadn't been able to tell me much but I was now aware that Laura had been one of the gaggle of school children who made a noise in Morelli's café each afternoon. Another morsel of information about her which made me realise how little I knew. I had never been aware of this collective meeting phenomenon, but it was difficult to ignore now I lived above the café and had nothing better to do at four p.m. I wondered if Laura had known Morelli's nephew. I should have asked Nicola if he hung about there two years ago; he certainly did now, causing giggling interest wherever he went.

The walk to Kelly's house took me to the other end of the town where the streets widened a little, so there was room for a grubby grass verge and a few skinny trees. In the dark damp evening everything looked bedraggled and forlorn. A light drizzle continued to spin beneath the street lamps. The street lamp which stood outside the Johnson house wasn't working. The bulb inside gave off a strange pink hue, haloing only its own lamp and distributing no light to the ground.

In front of number seventeen, what would have been a small front garden had been altered with gravel to make a parking space, but there was no car. A narrow line of light pierced through, between the drawn curtains of an upstairs room. I approached the door and rang the bell. Through the chime I thought I heard movement but nobody came to the door. I pushed the bell again and listened, my ear pressed against the door but there was nothing. My feet crunched the gravel as I walked a little way down the side of the house towards the shut garage. A motor bike, covered with a grey tarpaulin, was parked by the back gate but no evidence anybody was at home. Finally, I returned to the front door and looked through the letter box. There was a neat hall, an open door to the kitchen but nothing else. I let the shutter close with a clang. Perhaps the Johnsons didn't live here anymore.

Turning to go I had the uncanny sense of being watched. I turned back quickly and was sure there had been a movement of one of the curtains. I could have been imagining it but I didn't think I was. Whoever was there wasn't going to speak to me.

Chapter 7

It was late afternoon, the Saturday shoppers making their way home. The misery of the day still hadn't lifted and seemed to pervade everything and everybody. Even the few people still about were dull, with their dark coats and jackets, hunched like scuttling animals under thick carapaces. The sky hovered between a loath dusk and night black in an ominous cauldron of dark and darker shifting cloud cover. I remembered that the police search had been mid-morning. I had heard nothing about the results. It was as though the population had not yet returned. The town was too quiet, as if everybody that could had deserted and those forced to stay had been bewitched into a sinister muteness. My footsteps sounded hollow over the stones.

Suddenly there was a shout.

"Philip!" It was so unexpected that it took me a moment to recognise my name had been called. It came again, a wailing that extended my name.

"Phil….ip!"

Finally I turned to see a colourful blur rushing towards me like a displaced rainbow.

"Are you ignoring me?" asked Marti, reaching my side and slightly out of breath.

"No. Of course not."

"How are the photographs going?"

"I've taken them, but I need to do some adjustments to the prints," I said, thinking about my pictures in D. I. Russell's hands. The one of the bracelet was probably pinned up as evidence in the police unit. I didn't think Marti needed to know that.

"Come and have a cup of tea with me," she said and added, "you look as if you could do with one."

She slid her crimson clad arm through mine with a firmness that made it clear that a refusal was not an option. She seemed surprisingly small walking beside me. I did not think Marti was a large woman but she draped herself with so many layers of soft colourful fabric that somehow she took up space.

Even her dark hair was edged with scarlet but it suited her so naturally she could have been born with it. Her mouth was painted with glossy red lipstick; I had a sudden pleasant notion of kissing her, but did not.

We walked down the road until we reached her shop. There was an intricate calligraphy 'closed' sign on the main door and we took the alley alongside the shop to enter by the side door. Beside the door was the head of a terracotta figure, a man's face peering out of a garland of oak leaves. His expression was one of vigilance. A Green Man watching over Marti's visitors.

Stepping through the entrance brought us in at the back of the shop behind the serving till and storage boxes. It was gloomy space until Marti flicked the light switch. Instantly, my senses were overpowered as if I had had stumbled upon an oasis of colour, smell and gentle noises.

There was a flight of shallow steps and I followed Marti down, pushing aside green velvet drapes which concealed the door into the back room. The space was simply furnished with a scrubbed wooden table and chairs. The walls were white washed and there was wooden shelving and a Welsh dresser rather than any kitchen units. On the dresser I could make out the shapes of curved ornaments and crockery. Everything was smoothed and rounded. There were no hard edges or squared utensils, even the quarry tiles on the floor were eroded into a softly contoured landscape. It was not strange the room seemed so basic and functional; I had been in here before and knew this was Marti's work space, away from the shop.

It was quite dark and Marti lit candles in wall sconces and they flickered and hissed for a few moments adding to the buttery smoothness of the room's contents.

I hesitated near the entrance, reluctant to sit down due to the object in front of me. On the centre of the table was a glass ball. It gleamed like a reflection of the moon, its silver lucidity balanced on a dark wooden block. I did not want to look at it, afraid of what writhing visions I might see in it. I hoped Marti wasn't considering it either.

Marti filled the kettle, switched it on and turning back indicated with a nod of her head that I should sit. Without question I obeyed and she came and sat opposite me at the table. She said nothing.

"It's a lovely object," I said nodding at the glass globe, watching the candle flames reflected and moving within it giving the illusion of goldfish swimming in a glass bowl.

Marti simply smoothed its surface with the palm of her hand as if she was stroking a cat. Then she picked it up with both hands and gazed at it with a smile and look of wonderment, the same way one might look into the eyes of a new born baby. In an effort to dissuade her from telling me what she saw, I asked, "How can a glass ball tell the future?" My tone was deliberately antagonistic.

She seemed unaffected by the attitude in my voice and kept looking at the sphere.

"It's the nature of glass."

She turned the ball slightly, peering a little more closely at it. I leant forward too, and saw a tiny reflection of myself suspended upside down, moving as I moved, beneath its surface.

"Glass is not a true solid." She continued tilting the orb between her palms. "Some say it is a super-cooled liquid. That would mean it had a capacity for ebb and flow, like a moon pulling the tides."

She tipped it again so I expected to see figures and air bubbles move in it like a shaken snow globe.

She turned and placed the crystal ball carefully on the side adjusting the stand under it with precision as if it were necessary for it to be in an exact position. And speaking to the globe rather than me she said matter-of-factly, “It is not the time for crystal balls though.”

Marti was not beautiful in a conventional sense; she did not have high cheekbones, fantastic eyes or a perfect mouth, but everything about her had warmth, from the brown eyes to the freckled skin and the flush on her cheeks.

In the past I had always tried to avoid her. I knew she was great friends with Sarah and I had no doubt Sarah shared confidences with her. I had always been a little concerned about the domineering effect she had on Sarah, but now I felt it too, the need of a person chilled to the bone to draw close to the warmth of the hearth.

She reached out and took my hand in hers. Her hand was soft and plump; I was aware of my bony, cold fingers.

“You need help,” she said softly. Her eyes were kind, the room warm. It felt safe. I wanted to curl up and fall asleep for a long time.

She turned my hand over and started stroking my palm; I made no effort to resist. Her fingers followed the lines etched into the leathery skin.

“So much sadness here,” she said.

“You don’t need to read my palm to know that.” I grumbled and pulled my hand away sharply.

When I looked up she was smiling good-naturedly.

The kettle whistled and steam pumped into the air. Marti got up. I rested my hands back onto the table but they were pale and stiff against the wood as if they had been abandoned. The wood was smooth with age, my fingers adding an alien harshness to the room.

Marti was busy for a few minutes. It appeared she was taking trouble spooning out a specific amount of tea leaves into a pot and then waiting before pouring the water in.
She placed a wide white tea cup in front of me and the steaming liquid streamed in, dark tea leaves swirling round in the golden current.

I looked at it suspiciously.

"This is tea? I usually prefer mine strong, made from a tea-bag, with plenty of sugar and milk added."

"Yes, well that may be what you do usually, but today we need to read the leaves."

"Seriously?"

"Absolutely. This tea tastes great anyway."

"What is it about tea?" I muttered as I took the first hot sip.

"Ah," she said. "Tea is ancient medicine. It is the essence of the bush it grows from. It is the liquor of nature."

"So is beer then or whisky," I replied obstinately.

"If you like." She nodded, not troubled. "The thing with tea though, unlike alcohol, is that it enhances the senses rather than detracts from them with drunkenness."

I couldn't answer that. I knew all too well about inebriation.

The tea did taste nice. It had a refreshing bitterness to it that quenched my thirst. I was aware of Marti watching me as I drank. I concentrated on the tea and looked at the black debris moving about as if ready to settle my future. As soon as I had drained the last drop of fluid Marti took the cup from me in both hands. She stood up, the candlelight illuminating her into a priestess, and she turned the cup swiftly upside down onto the saucer.

"Now you turn it," she ordered. "Three times."

I did as she asked. Usually I would be cynical about such things but tonight it was entertaining. It had been so long since I had been in the company of an attractive woman, the novelty made me want to laugh. I could not remember the last time I had watched television or seen a show. The few occasions I had laughed were at the Talbot when I'd drunk too much and the world and his wife were suddenly amusing.

So I kept a straight face and turned the cup, resisting the urge to chant 'abracadabra.'

Obviously I was not a good actor.

"Try and take this seriously Philip, you might learn something," Marti chided.

She picked the cup up carefully and settled back in her chair. She was silent for some time whilst she turned the cup. The candlelight flickered over her, the red in her hair creating a blaze.

"Well," she said at last, putting the cup down. "This is interesting."

And instinctively, unable to help myself, I leaned forward reaching for the cup, needing to see what she had seen.

She leaned back closing her eyes momentarily.

"You've lost something."

"That would be Laura?" I said disappointed; for a moment I had thought I was going to hear something useful.

"No, this is more recent, the pain is very intense. You feel abandoned."

I thought of Sarah and Mac together, and indeed the ache in my heart seemed to tear the tissue.

"You're also looking for something. It's obscure though." She gave me a questioning frown.

"What is it you're about to do?" She looked directly at me. I had the feeling she was talking about the experiment but I wasn't yet sure that I was ready to tell her.

Her stare unsettled me, her eyes almost black in the candlelight as if they were bottomless wells drawing secrets into their depths.

"I know it's something that will cause trouble, but," she continued, putting the cup down, "then I see calm."

She looked at me again her gaze now gentle, the eyes returned to brown. Perhaps she had hypnotized me or drugged me with the tea but I found myself telling her. I told her everything. About the experiment, how Mac had first made a comment about Mary Queen of Scots and if I could, I might be able to find Laura's ghost.

As I explained it to Marti she sat quite still, listening and non-judgemental, and I realised if anybody would understand she would. At the end of my explanation I still said, "It sounds insane, I know," so if she wanted she could agree.

"Maybe it is insane, Philip, but this is simply your way of closure. After a tragedy like Laura's death, some people would have turned to religion, others to their work; you need a way to express your grief."

I wanted to tell her that it wasn't simply about grief.

"People will think you are mad, though. You need to take care."

I shook my head at her. "It can't harm anyone."

"People have been burned at the stake for less." She said it so seriously, her soft features hardened in a frown, as if capital punishment still existed.

"Nobody need know, anyway." And suddenly I felt panic rising, that Marti might reveal what I had just said, to the only person it could hurt. "Don't tell anybody. Don't tell Sarah." I hoped Mac wouldn't say anything to her either, but I suspected he was less of a risk. "She'd only worry."

We were silent for a time, just watching each other and the way the moving candle light changed our features. Suddenly Marti broke the quiet.

"You're a Cancerian aren't you, Philip?"

I nodded wondering where she had got that information. I vaguely remembered Sarah having a horoscope chart drawn up for us as a romantic anniversary gesture years ago. I thought at the time Marti had concluded our astral destiny had been 'soul mates'. I wasn't about to argue the point with Marti now.

"Your moods move with the path of the moon," she continued.

"And what's the moon doing at the moment?"

"It's on the wax. It was a new moon last Friday. That would be a time of revelation. Now life will be more of a struggle until the Full Moon at the end of next week. That will finish the cycle."

She put her hands flat on the table as if pressing something firmly into place. I noticed that her fingernails were painted purple.

The room had become cool, the evening outside black. I was aware of the rattle of rain on the windows.

Marti stood up and cleared the crockery from the table. She blew out all but one of the candles, the smoke writhing at their demise. With the last candle she lit a small lamp, and the flame flickered behind its glass like a dainty, bright bird. Then she came over to me and took my hand. With slight pressure she pulled me from my chair. I followed her upstairs, recognising the vague premonition about kissing her I'd had, when I first met Marti in the miserable afternoon, was about to be fulfilled.

Upstairs the simple décor of the downstairs room was violently contrasted. Rich coloured drapes and curtains embellished everything, the soft orange lamplight enriching it. The air was heavily scented with a lush fragrance like a summer garden. Her bed was a four poster, with a thick eiderdown shimmering with embroidered flowers. We fell onto it smiling and kissing. I had been in a drought from physical affection and as we touched each other on the silken fabric I felt I was being drenched in a sensual monsoon. I was nourished by every lick and kiss. Enriched by every murmur or sigh. But mostly each touch and caress made me warm. It was as if we had escaped February and rolled into summer.

As I peeled layers of clothing away and touched her body, my frozen fingertips seemed to hiss against her skin like melting ice. My tongue followed the salted contour from the downy hollow of her arm pit around the pale moon mound of breast. My lips sealed round her nipple which became firm in my mouth and I felt the pleasant weight of my erection stiffen as she stroked my skin. Above her hip bone she had a birthmark, a brown swirl like a knot in wood; I pressed the tip of my tongue against it enjoying the contrast of its irregularity amidst the smooth flesh of her belly. I caressed the moist fold of her groin leading me towards the dampness below the soft mound of coiled dark hair. I plunged into her warm folds and felt the responsive pressure pull me in and heard Marti's low moan. My body was drawn to the brink between exquisite heat and intense ice that bounds the perimeter between pleasure and pain. The thrill moved through me, igniting forgotten circuits of my whole being.

And as the pleasure became almost unbearable my head became satiated with summer light; I could feel its warmth on and under my skin. In the distance I heard the distant throb of a sprinkler turning and imagined a rainbow caught in the arc of its spray. I sensed each water droplet being absorbed into the parched earth. I was aware of noise in the air as if heavy bees laden with nectar from succulent flowers were lazily moving about. My tongue tasted honey. I became small, a minute observer sitting within the glorious bowl of satin flower petals about to open. I unfurled with them. I could hear them creaking open, green gates swelling towards the sun and bursting into flower. Then the rain came. Unleashed, like a warm shower drenching everything with its cleansing moisture. It pooled in the hub of the flower and I was immersed in it. Light and warmth and colour permeating every thought and every movement.

Finally we became still. We lay like sunbathers naked and side by side, staring up at the blue swathe of fabric that canopied the bed.

Only at the sound of her voice did I realise I was nearly asleep.

"Philip," she said again.

"Mm," I sighed, turning towards her my arm reaching out lazily to caress her breasts.

"Where were you on Wednesday evening?"

I murmured the word, "Wednesday." It seemed so distant, I had difficulty recalling it.

"Probably in the pub." But after a moments thought, as wakefulness edged in, I realised I hadn't been. "No. I was home. Researching the experiment. Why?" I added, thinking how peculiar the question was.

"Would you do me a favour?" I didn't need to say anything, we both knew I would.

"If anybody asks, just say you were here with me."

"Why? What have you been up to," I smiled sleepily and kissed her lips briefly.

"Nothing really. You'd just get me out of an awkward situation."

Momentarily, I wondered why Marti might be asking me to cover for her. She was somebody who didn't lie, yet she was asking me to lie for her if needed. The chink of mistrust was uncomfortable and I was in a state of mind I didn't want to disturb. Who was going to ask me about Marti's whereabouts anyway? It was pleasing to pretend I had already spent another night with her.

I kissed her more deeply, sealing my promise.

The following morning I awoke burrowed snugly under the sheets. Marti was not there. I guessed it must be late. The daylight was sharp as if the previous night's rain had washed the sky clean.

I ran myself a bath adding some green liquid that gave off an exotic scent. It was not a floral perfume but a rich woody aroma as if delicate stems had been crushed. A picture of dark beautiful women rolling tobacco leaves along their smooth thighs wafted into my thoughts. I held the image whilst I lazed in the bath, luxuriating in the foaming deep water, wondering how a man could survive with a pathetic shower and no sex for so long.

I could imagine every cell of my body renewing itself with vigour. My blood circulation that had been so sluggish, pumped round by a grief-damaged heart, had a pulse again.

I finally dragged myself out of the bath and dried myself on Marti's thick towels that held her lingering musky scent. Even my ragged reflection looked back at me with a smile from the steamed mirror. Perhaps the battered mirror in my flat was a black and white version because in Marti's bevelled looking-glass I had my colour back. A healthy pink shaded my cheek bones and the blue of my eyes was bright. I had once been considered good-looking; for a moment that man had returned.

As I left quietly later, I could hear Marti moving about in the shop. I didn't go and say goodbye in case the spell of our time together would be broken. I crept out by the side door.

The café seemed busy as I walked across the square. The aroma of Sunday breakfasts wafted from some distance away. The smell was mouth-watering and the condensation on the windows a suggestion of the warmth inside. However, I was still wrapped up in the blanket of Marti's tenderness and I ignored the hum of conversation and promise of sociability. For once I felt quite content with my own company. I may have been humming as I walked through the back gate. My happy mood and path was temporarily blocked. Sitting on the steps up to my flat was

Morelli's nephew. He was busy tapping messages into his phone and didn't look up until I was standing on the step below his flashy trainers. He observed me with an amused expression on his handsome face, willing me to confront him. Briefly I considered asking him if he had known Laura, but his insolent smile suggested he would delight in tormenting me rather than tell me the truth. I resisted the urge to kick out and simply squeezed past him taking care not to touch the black leather of his jacket. I could feel his arrogant stare follow me right to my door.

My flat greeted me like an ignored rubbish dump.

There were a couple of dirty mugs in the sink, and on the table books remained open, giving off a slightly musty odour, as if they had been respiring whilst I had been away. I was reminded of what I was supposed to be doing. I had allowed myself to be side tracked from my mission. I couldn't be too unhappy about the distraction but I needed to get back on with my task of uncovering ghosts.

I still had to decide on a developer to paint on the stairs of the Talbot hotel. One which might process a ghost. My brain seemed slow as if it was still engulfed by a residual humidity from last night. I decided to walk.

Morelli's nephew had gone when I left.

My feet took me down my usual route to the woods. It was the place I felt closest to Laura. The final place she had warmth and thought and feeling.

A fine drizzle had started to fall but I ignored it. I was still swimming with the warm memory of last night and trying to consider the next stage of the experiment.

The by-pass traffic was quite heavy as I waited to cross, the winter grime on the vehicles dulling their shine. The black BMW was an exception, gleaming like jet, the rain shimmering off it. As it passed I thought it slowed down, throwing water up at me from the edge of the road. I stepped back to avoid the wing of spray.

Finally, I crossed to the fields, the white of the mill hazy in the distance, everything muted by the mist of rain.

A lone seagull wheeled and called across the damp countryside, as if it had been displaced. It was a pale grey shadow against the pewter sky. Like a lost soul its cry filled the wide expanse of air. Like me, seeming to crave answers.

As I passed the mill, the trails of police ribbon flapped, a bedraggled red and white that marked this place as somewhere of note. There were traces of it as I moved into the wood. Most of it had broken or torn so it gave the effect of tatty bunting that had been long forgotten after whatever celebration had occurred. It snapped as the wind snared it and whipped it into tendrils which caught and tangled in the low branches.

I found myself leaning on the wooden bridge among the familiar trees. A musky remnant of Marti's perfume briefly drifted from my jacket and my thoughts returned to the night before. I closed my eyes and remembered the comfortable sound of rain on the windows blocked out from our sweet circle of warmth under the blue canopy.

But I was allowing myself to be distracted again. Forcing my eyes to open, I ordered my senses to assimilate information from my surroundings. The wood was like a vast cauldron. I was reminded of school dinners. The trees about me made sounds like the scratch and hum of stainless steel against pots and pans in kitchens, with the warm fug of decomposing cabbage lingering, echoing the similar smell of the woodland. I listened to the rain filter through the leafless canopy and smelt the woody amalgamation of leaves and debris below me. The bridge was more a walkway that covered a ditch. It was usually dry or simply a muddy furrow. Today though, a trickle of water had manifested itself, struggling through the brown debris that had collected in the gully staining the worm of water russet. It made a vague rustle as is crept over moist leaves.

Leaves and water. Water and wood. The words drummed themselves into my head with a percussion of precipitation dripping in the background. Leaves and water. Water and wood.

Suddenly I had it.

The vague memory of my meeting yesterday, of hands and warmth and the future. Ice melting. An inspiration came to me as if my brain was absorbing the idea like blotting paper.

A crazy notion. A brainwave generated from a madman's mind. I could almost hear the sizzling of neural pathways within my skull as if liquid was sizzling on a hot plate.

Tea.

What if I made a blend of tea from the oak leaves and brewed it with water into a developing solution?

The dripping continued around me, rustling the branches. It had an element of hilarity about it. Ignoring the mocking, I continued my train of thought. The tea would be a concentrated version of the chemicals that bound the spirit in the wood, and like a reel of film the picture would be revealed by increasing the concentration.

As I looked to the trees, their branches exposed, and down to the brown mush on the ground, I realised my idea would have to be modified. The trees were bare.

Bark. The bark was still there; after all it was not a drink I was making, just a potion. I shuddered. It had not struck me before, but the thought of making a potion gave me the sensation I was stepping over a boundary of scientific experiment into magic.

The wind had gradually increased so the thin branches above me rattled in an antagonistic warning, stirring the air. It caused the rain-edged light to strobe across the tree trunks making the rough ridges ripple and writhe. Amidst the movement of shadow the graffiti heart stood out on its oak trunk like an island of calm. It hit me then. I had not appreciated the significance of those two letters, side by side, the first time I had seen them.

The initials. E.S. Emma Sutton.

So there was another clue that Emma had been here. Here, with somebody. Sweethearts meeting and inscribing the tree with a lasting motif of their love. Who? The second set of initials was unfinished giving no clue. And now Emma had vanished. Disappeared without trace. At least I had had a body to bury. It was some kind of closure. But just to disappear like that. The raw organs in my body started to sting again as I tried to put myself in the position of her poor parents. The pain became too great and I could not. My own agony at Laura's death tore at me again. My sobs were covered by the movement of branches and I brushed tears onto the sleeve of my jacket.

Perhaps I had been intoxicated by the fermentation of the wood around me, but I found myself wandering and stumbling between the bushes, moving branches, searching. I couldn't really expect to find anything. The police had already done a thorough search and they had been helped by the public to cover a wider area. To my knowledge, nothing more had been found. Still, I comforted myself with the idea that this was for Laura. I could assuage my guilt at my ineptitude in her accident. Helping with Emma's disappearance might make me feel better.

After stumbling about for some time amongst the dripping shrubbery I realised there was nothing. No more clues. I was powerless. Powerless to do anything about Emma, just as I had been powerless to stop Laura's accident. The only thing I could do was to carry on my experiment.

So, I began picking bits of bark off the oak tree. A desperate man foraging for truth. Peeling away layers of covering. My fingers teased at the rough edges of the bark, it came off with difficulty, coming away in various shapes, revealing bugs that scuttled away as their dwelling was demolished. Then I remembered I had a penknife in the depths of a pocket somewhere and scrabbled around for it. It had a flat, thin blade, quite useful for the miniature screws on camera equipment. The sharp implement helped ease the rough woody skin off the tree. I felt guilty as I exposed pale moist flesh below. It gave me a sensation of abuse as if I was molesting it.

I was so engrossed in my work that the scuffle I heard was just another woody noise I ignored.

"What are you doing, Mr. Lockley?"

I jumped and a splinter stabbed under my thumb nail. I winced as I turned. The knife fell to the ground between us. His voice was not loud but seemed to reverberate amidst the tall trees as if they had been disturbed too.

D. I. Russell looked at me levelly and I suddenly had the reverse image in my mind. The dishevelled, soaked man scraping at a tree, and the cool detective, his hair perfectly combed, practical in his strong black brogues, black leather gloves and rain coat. No wonder he looked at me with contempt.

"Just doing some research," I bluffed, pushing the piece of bark from my hand into my jacket pocket, which was already bulging with tree bark. Conscious of the tree dirt on my palm I tried to wipe it on my jeans, blood smearing from my stabbed thumb into the fabric with the rusty stain of bark. Russell just looked at me. I knew he was questioning my sanity but perhaps did not have the words to phrase the question. I wasn't sure of the law concerning removal of tree bark. I decided it could not be a criminal offence because the detective looked as if he would have enjoyed arresting me at the merest provocation.

Russell took a step towards me and my first reaction was to take one in retreat but that would have meant pressing against the tree. I held my ground. Russell was looking at the knife on the muddy earth. It glinted with the wash of rain oiling its surface. The handle was facing away from me. The smiling face of my mother-in-law swum in front of me. She had a superstition about dropped knives. Something about friendship and deception or promises being broken. I could not remember it. Russell bent and picked up the knife, with his gloved hand closing gently around the handle. He passed it to me blade first. There was an element of Russian roulette about the scene. As he dropped the knife into my outstretched palm I sensed fortune ebbing away.

After he had handed me the treacherous object he took one stride, almost gliding, so he was beside me. He put the palm of his gloved hand against the tree bark. Then the detective turned to the tree and placed one finger on the corner of graffiti heart and traced its outline. I shuddered at the vulgarity of the motion.

"E.S." the detective said heavily. "I wonder whose initials those are?" He turned to face me.

I said nothing and a minute of silence past except for the murmuring woody audience.

"Emma Sutton, I would guess. What do you think Mr. Lockley?"

"Possibly."

"Very possibly, I would say. And you were trying to get rid of it, weren't you?"

"No. I wasn't taking the bark from there, just from here, look!" and I pointed to the tender bareness of the patch I had revealed. My gritty fingers looked foul and stained beside the taut sleekness of the detective's constrained digits.

"Perhaps you were just about to remove the evidence of Emma's initials when I disturbed you. Were you worried that she had carved your initials after all?"

"No!" I shouted loudly.

Heavy footsteps came quickly towards us.

"Are you alright sir?" came the call of the young, female officer.

"Yes. I've finished here, Barton."

He turned and walked away, seemingly able to escape the drops of rain splashing from the branches.

I followed after a few minutes but could see the black BMW still parked at the roadside. It made me uneasy. They were watching me. I put my head down and walked briskly towards the river.

Chapter 8

On Monday, having nothing better to do I caught a bus into Kettering and made my way to Fernlea Residential Home to visit Sarah's Dad.

I had always got on with him reasonably well, although initially his manner had been gruff. When Sarah and I had first been going out I suspected he thought it wouldn't last. When he realised we were serious he would have short interrogative conversations with me, like a protective dog barking warnings when I came to collect Sarah to take her out. I must have passed the test because, finally, when Sarah and I declared we wanted to marry, he nodded and actually smiled. "You'll do, lad," was all he said in way of a blessing.

At that time Sarah's mother Eileen had still been alive. She was the talker in the family. Not that she chattered unnecessarily or gossiped. In fact, I don't think I ever heard her say a bad word against another person. It was just that she knew when to speak and what to ask, so that she'd draw conversation out of you like a spool.

Had she been around when Laura had died, Sarah and I might have had a chance of reconciliation. Eileen would have known how to talk about Laura and death. I could see us all sitting at the solid farmhouse table, grouped around it, maybe even holding hands like a séance and Eileen would be talking and listening like a medium channelling our grief. But without her we were islands. Unable to interact. With no method of communication.

I didn't mind travelling by bus though it seemed to me that it was another reminder of my failure as a human being in not having a car.

Still, it was a pleasant enough way to travel. Looking across the rolling countryside, the towers of numerous spires which Northamptonshire is known for, pointed at the mottled grey sky.

The bus driver was chatty. He took up conversation with an elderly lady muttering about the weather and spring and generally passing the time of day. I didn't contribute to the conversation but smiled at the less cynical picture of humanity the chatter portrayed. It may be called 'small talk', but for those of us swirling on the rim of society, it could be a big thing in making us feel less alienated from the hub of humankind.

Fernlea had once been a grand Victorian building that would have at one time been a wonderful residence, but now struggled to contort itself into the building it needed to be to accommodate twenty elderly and frail residents whilst meeting various demands from the health and safety council.

Unusually for him, Jim was sitting down stairs in the large lounge surrounded by other residents, mainly female. More often, he would be found in the smaller lounge, but of course I had not seen him for some time.

The young carer showed me in and said fairly loudly, "Jim, it's Philip to see you."

He turned his face towards her, his watery eyes taking time to focus.

"Okay, you don't need to shout," he said grumpily.

"How are you then, Jim?" I questioned as I pulled a smaller chair to sit beside him.

"What?" he responded moving his head to look at me. "Oh, it's you. They didn't tell me you were coming."

"I didn't know myself until this morning. Sarah sends her love."

"So what have you been doing with yourself, lad?"

"This and that," I hedged. "How about you?"

"Bloody awful, lad. They cut my hair this morning." He put his hand up to brush the white shorn stubble. "Bloody mess they made and I smell of women's perfume. And I've got to sit in this bloody lounge until lunch."

I felt sorry for him.

Some faces don't lose their good looks even in old age and Jim had that kind of face. A strong-boned, handsome face. The bite of wind had weathered the skin over the decades but the flesh, although lined, had remained taut.

"Too hot in here," he said, truthfully. His big hands rubbed the fabric of his trousers. He seemed agitated. I watched them as they moved. They hadn't become knotted and skeletal with time but remained spade-like. Hard-working hands, the skin toughened to a leathery sheen.

"So what you been doing with yourself then, lad?" he repeated at me.

"Not much," I said absently, a little concerned about him. I knew I wasn't the most cheerful companion, nor the most interesting, but this grumbling, repetitive man was not the usual Jim.

I looked through heavy drapes to the fragment of grey scudding cloud visible between the crammed in walls. It seemed unfair to house a country man in a home without a view. Sarah and I had done our best to find Jim somewhere suitable when he needed residential care after a fall, but I suddenly felt guilty that I had abandoned him to such a miserable glimpse of sky. There had been a garden until last year when they had built over the green tree-edged space and reduced it to an anonymous parking area leaving a tiny square of gravel and pot plants, saying the garden had been little used and the upkeep disproportionately expensive. We wrote several letters requesting the garden be kept but obviously were in a minority.

"Let's go out," I said suddenly making my decision and standing up.

"What?" said Jim, "Go out?" He looked at me with an expression as if not believing he had heard correctly.

"Yes." I nodded.

"That would be grand." He smiled, the grumpy façade instantly wiped away.

It took an age for somebody to find a wheel chair and move Jim from the deep armchair. He needed the bag on his leg adjusting and I was advised on what he could do and where we should go.

When I said "We'll have our lunch out" I was given another five minutes of advice before they let us leave, but they seemed happy to have one less responsibility for a while.

I decided not to push him down to the park. The going would be fine but coming back up the hill later might be a struggle. After consulting Jim we decided on the cemetery.

"I'll be there soon enough, permanently, lad," grumbled Jim, only half joking.

I didn't patronise him with the usual platitude. Jim was a man who preferred straight talking. Not only had I grown accustomed to his manner over time but as Laura grew I recognised she had a similar candour, a trait of stating the facts.

We slowly moved down the wide path between the various memorials. Plain stones, simple crosses and more ornate pieces. The choices, of course, more to do with the people burying the dead than the bodies below. Most of the monuments were weathered and worn but considering some of the dates inscribed they showed a resilience to the world that the corpses beneath had been denied. Some memorials had vases of flowers, others were completely bare as if either nobody bothered to visit or there was no one left to care, and on some plots nearer to the low enclosing wall, nature had added her own mossy embellishment. Any flowers that were there all appeared faded as if they knew this was not the place for floral exuberance and had toned down their vividness in response.

"Do you ever visit, Eileen, lad?" Jim asked, as we watched a woman kneeling and refreshing the flowers by a gravestone. Even this fresh bouquet suddenly took on an air of pallor as it was laid against the cold stone.

"Yes. And Sarah takes flowers"

Eileen was buried in the same cemetery as Laura, in Oundle. It was one of the reasons Sarah had been adamant she wanted Laura buried rather than cremated; I think it was a small comfort to her that Laura was near her Grandmother and not totally alone.

"Do you ever see her ghost?" The question surprised me as I asked it. I had not meant to, and waited for a short sharp reply.

"Nah, lad. Don't believe in that stuff." He said it adamantly, and I thought that would be the end of the matter. But after a moment of silence, in which I presumed he had been thinking about his dear departed wife, he continued in a softer tone.

"At first I nearly drove myself mad. Kept seeing glimpses of her." He spoke quietly, and I wondered if he'd ever confided the information to anyone else. I imagined it would be difficult for him to admit. He made a gulping sound as if even after all this time he had to hold back tears.

"It took me a while to accept she wasn't coming back. But I never saw her actual ghost. She was such a good person, why would she be sent to haunt me here? It's the memories I have of her that will remain always. She lived a good life, she died a peaceful death."

We fell into silent thought again, ghosts of the past not visible but raised in our minds.

Making our way down the rows I spent a few minutes beside the beautiful carved angel gazing down protectively over my mother's grave. In the light I could quite clearly make out the carved script.

'Grace Lockley'
'Loving mother and wife'
1st Dec 1931- 20th July 1973

The memorial was the only thing Dad and I had ever agreed on. In the daylight the statue reminded me of Mum, the smooth complexion and the downward gaze, reluctant to show anybody the pain she was suffering. The afternoon light tinged the stone, casting grey planar shadows. It resembled my mother's unhealthy pallor.

I used to read to her, sometimes from the newspaper and other times books and plays; it depended on her mood. This was where the seeds of my future career in journalism were planted. I would sit at the foot of her bed, my eyes straining due to the dimness of the light. The curtains were always partly drawn, keeping the sharp light which gave her headaches from mother's eyes. Every day she put a little make up and perfume on. But nothing completely covered the medicinal smell of the sick room.

I muttered an atheist's prayer and wandered back to Jim. If he noticed my preoccupation with this particular memorial or my pious mutterings he didn't say.

After we had mooched around in the chilly air for a time I pushed the wheelchair up the road towards the town and we stopped by a take away. I ordered fish and chips, neither of us feeling guilty that they were one of the forbidden foods mentioned by Jim's carers. We found a bench on the market square to eat them. Pigeons, realising that food was available, cooed nearer and nearer without fear.

"So, what you been doing with yourself, lad," Jim asked.

Finally I decided I ought to make more of an effort in conversing with Jim. He didn't need to know about trying to raise ghosts; I could expect a short, antagonistic retort to that kind of talk. But he might be interested in the experiment.

"I'm doing an experiment for an article," I white lied.

Jim stopped with a chip half way to his mouth. "Go on," he encouraged.

I remembered he had always been a craftsman. On the farm he had often tinkered with machinery and made things for the house.

"Well, I'm a bit stuck to be honest. I need to create a mild force field." I peeled off a bit a fish and enjoyed it flaking in my mouth.

"Why do you want to do that, lad?"

"Well, it's difficult to explain. I want to reproduce the sense before a storm."

"Sounds a bit daft to me, lad," Jim said with his usual bluntness.

Jim was of course a practical man. His inventions had always had a useful end point. He ate a chip with exaggerated chewing motions. When the mouthful had gone he continued, "It's not so difficult to do though."

He stopped and reached for another chip and chewed it thoughtfully. Because he didn't expand on the experiment I guessed he had forgotten my enquiry. We finished our meal in silence. I was aware of the cool, damp air and knew I should be getting Jim back to Fernlea.

Bringing our outing to a close, I got up from the bench and crunched up the fish and chip papers. I threw them in a nearby bin and wiped my hands against my jacket. Tucking the blanket more firmly around his legs I said, "Come on, let's get you home," and started to push Jim slowly back towards Fernlea.

"You'd need a source of high voltage and an antenna."

It took me a moment to realise what he was talking about and I stopped pushing. The wheelchair rolled back slightly. I didn't want to appear foolish but I needed advice, so I asked, "What would I need then?"

He seemed to give a grunt and didn't say any more. After waiting a few moments in the hope that he might continue I gave up. I started to push him again, feeling an ache develop in my shoulders from the uncommon exercise.

Just as we turned into the drive way he said, "You need the web, lad."

I stopped again, not following this conversation. Obviously, Jim sensed my slowness. "The world wide web, you know, computers. You can find anything on there."

For a second I wondered how he knew that but equally I knew he was right.

I pushed the wheelchair up the ramp to the entrance, considering how to get access to a computer.

After a brief goodbye and a promise I would be back to take him out again soon, I left Jim to the care of the nurses. As I made my way back to the bus stop I remembered the library. They would have computers there. It was late afternoon now but I guessed it would still be open.

Most modern libraries I presume are light buildings with echoes and voices and movement. This building was still in the dark ages. Entering into the claustrophobic hallway panelled with dark wood and the gloomy rooms made me feel as if I should be creeping about.

A girl who looked no more than a teenager looked up as I approached the desk. I coughed. I was scared of speaking, conditioned to the rule, 'one must be silent in libraries.' The girl smiled though and said in a normal tone, "Can I help you? Were you looking for something particular?"

"Well, I wanted to use a computer to do a web search."

"Sure," she said easily, "It's fifty pence for half an hour."

I scrabbled in my pocket and placed the coin on the desk. After a few moments the girl lifted an opening in the desk and turned, saying, "Follow me."

I did as she asked and we moved into a smaller area off the main library. There were a few desks, a couple of them occupied.

"Have you used the internet before?" she asked

"I have, but a while ago," thinking back to the last time I used a computer which must have been almost two years ago when I was still working.

"I'll log you on then and get you started."

She sat down and with ease clicked and tapped until the search box appeared.

"Now what did you want to search for?"

I hesitated. As always when the words you want to say might sound embarrassing the room suddenly seemed incredibly quiet, even more silent than the minute before, as though the people there had stopped even breathing.

I was just about to say, 'photographing ghosts,' but noticing my discomfort and taking in my shabby appearance, I guessed she was predicting I was probably pretty short on companions; she said in a loud whisper, "Was it a chat room?"

"No," I said with indignation. "Photographing ghosts."

She rolled her eyes and turned back to the screen. Either she suspected I was lying or she thought it more natural behaviour to be seeking friends rather than ghosts.

"Well, just type that in the box then. You have the option to search within the results if you need to. The link is at the bottom of the page."

She vacated the seat. "I'll leave you to it. Just ask if you need any assistance."

As she left the area she turned and said, "Oh, and we close at four today," looking pointedly at the clock on the wall indicating I had just under my paid for half an hour to sort this out.

I sat down in front of the screen. Though the basic set up was much as I remembered, it still felt an alien thing. I had never liked computers. The mouse jumped and bobbed under my unpractised palm, and it took me a few moments to put the words 'Photography Ghosts' in the search box. Instantly the screen was filled with options. In the top corner it stated 'Results 1-10 of about 1,250,000 for PHOTOGRAPHY GHOSTS (0.11 seconds).'

Now that was magic.

I wished I could have input the name 'Laura Lockley', and been shown millions of clips from Laura's life as instantaneously. My brain must have a catalogue of Laura memories stored away but somehow I couldn't access them with the same immediacy.

I flicked through the first few pages but nothing was reminiscent of what I was looking for. This could take days, and I still might not find what I wanted. I returned to the search screen and added 'techniques' to my search. Again the response was instantaneous. I looked at the search stats. Again there were over a million hits.

I scrolled down the page. About half way down I recognised the words. 'Kirlian Photography'. The phrase that had eluded me.

That's what Weird Wilf had gone on about; Kirlian auras and capturing them on print. He would say the technique showed the spirit within a natural object.

I manipulated the mouse to enter the site, aware of the time ticking away and of the other users scraping chairs back to leave.

There was so much information here and so many links I was never going to get through it all.

I started to read.

I had almost devoured the first page when the librarian came back and said, "Sorry, it's time to leave. I need to shut down all the computers."

I glanced back to the screen and saw a link high-lighted in pale blue.

'Tutorial article on Kirlian Photography. Building your own equipment.'

I had enough time to click the link and feel my spirits lift. I'd found exactly what I needed.

"Sorry, Sir but you really must leave now."

"Is there any way I can print this off? I really need this," I pleaded.

The girl sighed and looked at the clock, the hands moving past four o'clock.

"Black and white copies cost twenty pence for each A4 page."

I felt in my jacket pocket. Between my fingers was an ominous lightness of small change. Three pages were all I needed. Please let me have enough, I prayed.

I counted out pennies and five pence pieces; there was nothing larger than a ten pence piece in the pile. They totalled fifty-eight pence. I was left with a handful of dust and a grubby return bus ticket. I scrabbled in my pockets again but couldn't find the missing two pence. Shrugging in what I hoped was an endearing manner, I looked at the girl.

She sighed more loudly this time and shook her head, but said a resigned "Okay," as if she had become used to and tired of haggling with the likes of me. I pointed out the three precious pages I needed.

Minutes later I was outside clutching the plans for my dream apparatus. On the steps of the library I folded them small and pushed them into my inside pocket next to Laura's photograph. Then I walked quickly to the bus stop with my head bent against the cold wind and hoped I had not missed the bus. It was in view as I turned the corner, but the driver was helping a Mum on board with a baby, its buggy and several shopping bags, so I had enough time to run to it with seconds to spare.

I took my prized sheets out to look at on the bus but couldn't concentrate on them, so folded them up, impatient to get home.

Once safely in Oundle I scurried back home taking the steps up to the flat two at a time, a dangerous undertaking on the damp metal, but worth the risk today. I went straight in and sat down at the kitchen table and pushed everything aside so books and paper thumped and floated to the floor. I ignored them. Carefully I unfolded the pages and smoothed them as a man with a treasure map might caress the secret to his vision. It amazed me how in such a short time the papers could have become crumpled and raggedy. It seemed to be a gift of mine.

Still, I had them. I laid them side by side. On the first was a simple figure of the circuit with explanatory notes and on the second a photograph of how the device should actually look. It was perfect.

I reclaimed a scrap of paper from the pile on the floor and grabbed a pencil and started writing a list of what I needed.

It was a basic circuit so I needed batteries, wires, a base of wood and copper sheet for the discharge plate. Tomorrow, I would have to go to Paddy's store. Paddy owned the local hardware, electric, photo bits and 'everything you needed' kind of shop, the type of shop that only seemed to exist in smaller, more individual towns nowadays, able to throw off the 'identikit high street'. Paddy knew me pretty well and would probably let me have it on tick, which was also an advantage.

The problem was I needed something to do now to quell the excitement I felt. I might have some of the equipment in the studio. I was sure I had some photographic instrument batteries and possibly a piece of chipboard I could use for the base. I could go and have a look anyway.

I tucked the papers back into my jacket with the irrational fear that some one might sneak in and steal them whilst I was out and scuttled into the night.

When I got to Sarah's street I could see lights were on in the house and I was momentarily torn between knocking and telling her about my visit to her Dad or ignoring her. Driven by the adrenalin of discovery and desire to concentrate on the experiment, I decided on the latter.

As with most things rushed at, the usually simple procedure of finding a stored piece of equipment became problematic. Amongst the dust and rubbish pushed into the limited cupboard space created under a bench seat was string that had wound itself round every protruding piece of kit. The more impatient I became the more stubbornly it resisted.

The box I needed was stuck at the back of the cupboard. My hands were cold and after a time my back and knees hurt from kneeling down. Reaching in, I finally managed to rescue a muddle of things from the cupboard and sat on the cold hard floor. I concentrated on the mess like a determined child with a difficult puzzle, and finally untangled the box from its web. The catch was stiff and resisted opening but inside there were batteries and wire. I found some remnants of chipboard, probably from when the storage seat was made, pushed down the side of the cupboard. They would do.

Gathering a screwdriver, pliers and a few other tools in a bag, I snuck away like a burglar, the bag tucked under my jacket. Trying hard to be quiet I opened and shut the side gate slowly, but it threatened to give me away by squeaking loudly, and I wished I had remembered to oil it weeks ago.

I was pleased to see Ratty waiting for me when I returned. She emerged dry from behind the rubbish bins and followed me into the flat. In the kitchen I put down a saucer of milk for her. There was only a drop left in the bottle. I drank my coffee black.

My trawl didn't amount to much, and I realised that somehow I was going to have to try and sleep and wait for tomorrow.

Chapter 9

As early as possible I visited Paddy's. The outside of the shop was painted grey and inside the grey theme continued with utilitarian tools suspended from every available space. The shop was small and cluttered with objects so it was remarkable that Paddy knew where to find anything. I weaved my way through to the serving desk.

Paddy, clad in a grey overall, nodded at me in way of greeting. He didn't generally bother about idle chat. The only time I heard him have a conversation was when discussing a project of some sort.

I pushed the scrappy list and my now well thumbed pages across to him. "I want to make this. I've got the batteries."

He took in the figure and the photo of the finished device without comment, or any expression on his face. Taking a pen from the upper pocket of his overall he then began marking the list. He hesitated beside each scribble, some for a moment others for a little longer, and then made a dot. His mouth folded up in a gurning motion whilst he thought. I could almost see his mind flickering like a computer filing system registering where each item would be found.

He turned and disappeared into the back. I could hear drawers being opened and things being moved around.

Then he was back carefully placing the first items on the desk top. Gradually the small pile of treasure was added to until he nodded firmly at me, by way of a full stop.

"Can I pay you later in the month?"

Paddy nodded again as if he had been expecting the request. He wrote out a hand written receipt from a carbon pad, and put it and everything else in a brown paper bag. He smiled as he handed the bag to me. If he was intrigued by what I intended to manufacture he kept it to himself. He asked no questions and made no comment about the article.

I hurried back to the flat, intent on finishing the device as quickly as possible.

After a brief leap onto the table to check out what I was doing, Ratty requested to be let out, indignant that I had returned with a bagful of things which did not include food or milk.

The instructions were fairly straight forward and I found that quite quickly the random pieces began to resemble what was in the printed picture. I was reminded of playing with Meccano sets from years ago. A happy memory. It took me back to days before Mum's illness, even days when Dad had been around, helping with my constructions. I could feel that same sense of achievement ebb and flow. It must have been an awfully long time ago, so old the memories had a sepia glow to them.

Though not adept at physics, I had taken in most of the information about photography during my studies and I knew the set up for basic electrical circuits and the workings of camera equipment. I intended not to use the Kirlian device for contact printing, which was suggested, but would leave the discharge plate open to the air in the hope it would create a distended force field over the whole area of experimentation.

Everything else faded as I began work; the rumbling from the café below, the noise of pedestrians and traffic from the street, even the musty smell emanating from the bark pieces in their bowl. The wind was rattling the kitchen window pane in a conspiracy to discover what beguilement was taking place. I ignored all the distractions. I forgot about time, about food, about thirst. I removed myself to an alternative place of creativity.

Finally, I finished and sat back to admire my handiwork. The machine with its copper plate gleamed wonderfully amid the debris and tools of its manufacture. It looked like alien apparatus. I ran the test suggested, checking it was functional. The spark from the high voltage wire to the discharge plate was so bright and I was concentrating so hard that black smudges of light distorted my vision for several minutes.

I left the device ornamenting the centre of the table and got to work on the next stage of the experiment. Bark tea.

The wind was rising, the clattering against the panes more urgent, creating enough draught to move the curtains.

My culinary skills were minimal. It was a proficiency I had never learnt. When mother was ill I had opened and heated tins of soup for our tea. The habit had remained whilst I was a student. When working, my income had allowed the occasional take away to supplement my canned dinners. Then I married Sarah. My taste buds experienced such a change they could have been transplanted. Sarah did not cook fancy nouvelle cuisine but even so I thought I had reached a gastronomic heaven. I was fed regularly with a wide range of foods that had both texture and taste. I took it for granted. Now I was back to my specialities of soup and beans on toast.

There was an old saucepan in the back of the cupboard. I filled it with water, the electric ring glowing keenly beneath it.

Using the principle of making tea I simply added the bark pieces to the pan, dropping them in one by one each making a small splash, acoustic notches bringing me closer to my goal. 'Laura, Laura', they seemed to gurgle as the pieces submerged under the water.

Slowly the water began to boil. It darkened from soft grey to brown with froth forming at the edges. It smelt horrible. The aroma had a pungency to it that clogged my nasal passages. But it had a beneficial side-effect. It rid the flat of the final taint of D. I. Russell's aftershave. With the thought the smell became much more bearable.

When the liquor had reached a suitable depth of colour, taking on the tone of whisky, the window panes steamed with condensation, blocking out the day. I decided it must have reached a suitable potency. I drained the liquid through a sieve which had never been used in my tenancy. It filled an empty whisky bottle. The liquid looked suitably dark behind the label so I scratched out the name with a pen in case in a drunken stupor I might decide to drink it one night.

I placed the finished product beside the machine. Together they looked as if they were the artefacts of a religious act.

My job now completed, I felt hungry and tired. I raided the money for the electric meter to buy a fishcake and chips, and a pint of milk. Even with the threat of no electricity, my meal, accompanied by a mug of sweet, white tea was one of the best I'd had for a while.

It was not late but I decided to rest. I closed the thin curtains ineffectually against the brightness of the moon but it did not distract me. I slept soundly. It may have been the drug-like potency of the bark enriching the air which enabled me to sleep so well.

If I dreamt, they were calm dreams. The seeds of possible success were firmly implanted in my thoughts. I had put together the experiment and had no uncertainty I could succeed, firstly in raising the ghost of Mary Queen of Scots and then undoubtedly finding Laura.

I woke late to scudding skies, thin clouds racing across the expansive greyness. The agitation of the panes and movement of the curtains reminded me of the date. The 8th of February. The anniversary of Mary Queen of Scots' execution. As I remembered the significance of the day, I became buoyed with excitement. I didn't need the electric fire on; my body was generating its own heat. Finally my life had reason; it was something more than getting through the hours. I had an objective.

In this temporary place of contentment I naively dismissed any ideas of failure. I'd had enough of that in my life and I ignored the bitter shadow it tried to cast. I had become adept at doing that.

I had a tatty tartan suitcase I was going to use as a kit bag. I packed my equipment with the reverence it demanded; the coppery force field machine wrapped in layers of old newspaper, the bottle of liquor and a paint brush beside them.

The click of the old-fashioned clips of the case reminded me of summer vacations. I remembered the holidays I had been on as a child, simple trips to the seaside. Sand and ice-cream. The noise of the shutting case made me expectant of something I couldn't quite reach and instead was left with a sensation of regret, as if I were remembering a void.

Now I was ready. But with too much time to pass before the evening came, the shadow of possible failure started to encroach and I had to sit for a long time resisting the urge to fiddle with the contents of the case. Eventually darkness fell, and I clutched the handle of the suitcase and made my way into the café yard.

Chapter 10

It was already late by the time I walked into the bar of the Talbot Hotel. A couple of regulars were slouching by the fire but took no notice of my entrance. Mac took in my appearance and the suitcase I was carrying and said in mock seriousness, "Sorry we've no vacancies."

"Ha, bloody, ha," I responded equally dead-pan.

"Anyway, ye're more or less a stranger. You haven't been in here for a few days. My profits are goin' down."

Although he'd been the instigator of my Mary Queen of Scots mission, I guessed he'd forgotten about it or presumed I wouldn't go through with it. "I told you I'd be back on the eighth, with my experiment. This is all down to you, you know?" I reminded him.

"Ye'd better have a beer," Mac said, pulling the tap.

He placed the beer in front of me. I took a sip, appreciating the familiar smell and sweet taste against my dry lips. The sensation reminded me of Marti and I smiled imagining her arms around me keeping me warm. Abstinence certainly did make the heart grow fonder. I was about to tell Mac about my assignation last weekend. But I didn't. It might break the spell. And I did not want it getting back to Sarah.

"What have ye bin doin' then Philip?"

His tone was sharp and I thought somehow he had read my thoughts. I sat still, facing him, the glass held half way from my mouth and the bar top.

"Yer hands are filthy."

He continued shaking his head. I looked at my fingers grasping the glass and indeed under the short bitten nails was a curve of dirt from the tree bark and my fingers had been stained orange with tannin.

"My manicurist is ill," I answered, deciding not to tell him too much about my intended experiment.

For a time we were silent, the murmurs of the other customers in the back ground, Mac cleaning and tidying behind the bar.

Gradually the last customers drifted away.

Midnight is the hour for enchantment and I had decided not to break with tradition. So as the clock hands moved towards the appointed time I said as matter-of-factly as I could,

"I'll set my stuff up now, if that's O.K?"

"What did ye have in mind?" questioned Mac, a slight look of concern on his face.

"Well," I blustered with as much confidence as I could. "It's just this box here, and a developing solution."

Mac's frown deepened and for an awful moment I thought he was going to stop me. After a few seconds of consideration he shrugged.

"If ye do any damage, ye'll pay for it."

"Of course, Mac. It would be better if none of your guests were around though."

"There's only a few tonight. Ye should have the place to ye sen. I'll hang around in case ye need me."

"Thanks." Picking up the suitcase I slowly made my way into the hall like a reluctant actor.

At the base of the staircase I took out my machine. Even though it seemed smaller below the stairs than it had on my kitchen table, it still glimmered in the gloom beneath the dark oak.

Then with the paint brush I applied the bark solution to the banister. It dulled the wood but would not do it any harm. It would probably polish off.

I worked my way up to the first landing, making a thorough job of anointing the woodwork in the low glow of the lamps.

I returned the bottle to the bottom of the stairs and switched on the machine so a jagged spark of light leapt from the metal. It continued to emit a reassuring hum, like a bee contented with its endeavours.

The clock chimed twelve as I took up position half way up the stairs. Tonight I was sober. Sitting there seemed strange, with my thoughts clear, my elbows on my knees. Nothing to do but wait.

I was surprised Mac had let me go this far. Perhaps he thought it would exorcise the pain that encased me. Marti was right. This experiment had more to do with grief than anything else. Still, I had no where else to be.

Through the window glass in front of me, the moon hung like a crescent of silvery water casting dull light onto the stairs. I wondered how on earth I had ended up like this. Without alcohol the staircase was remarkably ordinary. The angles of the stairwell meant abstract shadows were cast, criss-crossing in a puzzle of darker and paler shapes.

I heard the occasional distant murmur or closure of a door; otherwise the stairwell was quiet. I would sit and think.

Reaching into my pocket I took out the crumpled photograph of Laura, and felt the familiar sting of happiness at seeing her smiling face only to remember she wasn't here. On the corridor above I heard a door shut and then footsteps. Some wandering guest was going to disturb me after all.

I was about to turn and make some excuse as to what I was doing loitering in the corridor at midnight, but an extreme cold draught made me hesitate. The air around became suffused with the smell of herbs and I could hear the swish of fabric. I did not dare look up.

Moments later I had the sensation of movement beside me, an envelope of cold pushing through the atmosphere.

A slim figure moved in front of me. She was wearing a long black dress, a white veil hanging down behind. Its delicate stitching was a web touching the carpet. The detail I could see was incredible. Then she appeared to hesitate, turning to grip the banister, her thin fingers bluish in the moonlight. On the front of her dress were tiny buttons in the shape of acorns. They glinted like bright eyes. The air thickened in a lucid fog and I could sense a stretching in the air as if caught between the ebb and flow of a tide. A tide of time ready to strike over and over again.

As she turned the corner of the stairs below me, I could see her pale face and pinched fine features. She held a book in her long fingered, milky hands, the colour of bone, and between them twisted mahogany beads. An agitated crucifix spun at the end. The small carved figure pressed against the crossed planks. The deftly sculpted ornament seemed alive with movement. The image of Christ's body struggling against his inevitable death seemed to resonate with the despair hanging about me. The heaviness of the air contracted leaving a claustrophobic airlessness. It was fear. I could hear its awful sound like the screech of breaking waves scouring pebbles to sand.

All around me there was the sensation of a terror about to occur. I could feel Mary's desperation but she kept walking steadily, nobly, her head held high.

I could not see her as she stepped into the hall, but she had been here. Not a dense real person that could have been flesh and blood, a joke Mac or Jamie might have set up, but a strong vision, real enough for me.

The photograph of Laura fell from my hands as my knuckles released their pressure. It swayed leaf-like through the banisters into the hall below. For a minute there was complete silence, then out of the darkness boomed a voice.

"Ye've dropped something, mate," came Mac's voice. His heavy footsteps began to come nearer, turning the corner of the stairs. He held the photo towards me. I reached to get it but could not control the shaking of my arm or dictate the movement of my fingers to take it from him.

"Are ye alright?" Mac said in a concerned voice, leaning down towards me to glare at my face, his voice sounding from far away.

"I saw her," I said weakly.

Mac patted a cold hand. "Yes, Yes," he soothed, his words and face coming into focus.

"I did. I saw Mary Queen of Scots," I said firmly.

As Mac helped me to my feet he remained silent and I sensed he had not seen what I had seen.

"I saw her," I repeated as I moved unsteadily still clinging to Mac's arm for support.

Again Mac was silent so when he did speak his words were a reprimand, as if I was a child inventing stories.

"I've bin standin' there ten minutes and I did'na see anything."

"I did. I saw her. Every detail," I responded, becoming the angry kid his words had suggested.

Mac led me down the stairs, back into the bar. Only the bar lights were on and the fire had burnt low, rustling a dull glow as if reluctant to go.

He poured whisky for us both and I took the glass gratefully, the brown glow warming my still shaking hands.

"Tell me then," said Mac, with a sigh.

"I saw her. The gown the lace, I even smelt herbs."

Mac nodded over my shoulder. "That's all in the painting."

He referred to the large oil painting hanging on the wall in the upper stage of the bar room. It was invisible in the darkness but I turned my head to look anyway.

"I bet you saw the wee doggy running at her heels."

"No. Just her. I saw details though, the acorn buttons on her dress. I saw her," I added firmly, becoming more agitated because Mac was obviously not convinced.

"Ye've bin reading about her, all of this it's just ye're imagination. Is it not?"

"No. No. I saw her, I saw her," I shouted, my head thumping with the desperation of not being believed. I turned and leant on the bar, my head held in my hands, to stop the infernal drumming. "You must have seen something," I demanded. "You've seen her before."

"I've never seen her, Phil. Just sensed a presence sometimes. But not tonight. I s'pose you might have seen something," he added reluctantly.

"I did. I saw her," I wept softly into my palms.

Mac put a hand on my shoulder.

"You're still shakin' man. I do na' think ye're well. Should I call someone?"

There was nobody else to call, so I didn't reply.

"Look I'll sort out one of the rooms for ye. I'm worried about ye. Phil ye need help."

I was hardly listening to him. My thoughts were churning. I had seen her. Did that make me mad?

Mac let me stay in one of the unused Hotel rooms. He had packed my experiment kit in its case and brought it to my room, where I lay coiled up, fully clothed, on the bed. Mac untied my shoes. He placed the trainers side by side on the floor. If he had removed the laces I would not have been surprised; I felt like a prisoner, unable to be trusted.

I did not sleep but watched darkness usurped by light. The thumping in my head had diminished to a disquietening hum.

Gradually, the shadows lifted and there was a gentle tapping on the door. At first I thought it might just be in my head, but the tap came again more firmly and Mac appeared at the door. As I turned to face him I knew my face was washed out. I could feel the swollen pouches of skin slung beneath each eye like the bruises of an inept boxer. My eyeballs felt rough and red. I suspected I did not look in the best of health.

Mac came into the room. His bulk blocked the gap in the door, but I knew somebody else was waiting there. He looked awkward.

"I thought ye should see a doctor," he finally spluttered. "I'm tha' sorry but I do na think ye're well."

I stayed where I was. The information took time to reach me as if his words were elongated and distorted in the space between us.

When I said and did nothing, Mac left, mumbling something to the doctor. The doctor came into the room, smart and efficient, pulling round the chair from the dressing table, and leaning towards me. Whether he was relieved or disappointed that I was not bouncing off the walls he did not reveal. He was professional, cool considering he had been dragged out this early.

"Your friend's very worried about you, Phil."

I immediately felt annoyed. Only a few people call me Phil and I hardly knew this man. He had introduced himself as he entered the room, but my brain was too muddled to absorb the information. Now I felt at a distinct disadvantage.

"I know."

"Do you know why?"

"I saw a ghost, that's all. A ghost that other people have seen. You don't have to come and cure them, do you doctor?"

I was still lying rumpled in my clothes. Over the years I had not had much to do with doctors. You only saw a doctor if you were really ill. I wasn't ill. Was I?

"I think he's been concerned about your health for a while."

"He was the one who started on about the ghost," I retorted like a sulky child.

"Maybe that's why. He's worried he might have triggered this reaction."

When I said nothing, the doctor continued.

"Episodes like this often build up over time."

"Episodes like what?"

"Hallucinating, hearing voices, that kind of thing. Sometimes these things can be prompted by upsetting events in our lives."

The doctor opened his medical bag and took out an instrument. He shone a light in my eye, making me wince. Brown smudges were left on my vision. They disorientated me.

He took my pulse. Like a puppet limb, my hand jerked upward as he gripped my wrist.

"Well, your vital signs seem in working order. Do you have a head ache?"

"No," I lied.

"It's probably stress related, an anxiety attack. Have you had any occurrences like this before?"

"I haven't seen a ghost before, if that's what you mean?"

I knew he did not.

"No," he responded calmly, "I meant visual occurrences, seeing things, blacking out, spots of light, difficulty focusing."

"No."

"As I said, these things can happen when we have to overcome problems in our life. Problems that we have no control over."

He was obviously referring to Laura's death. Mac must have filled him in on the details. I didn't want this stranger to know my business. Mac had no right to invite him here and discuss my personal life with him. I wished I had the strength to sit up and look prepared to face the world. Trying to lurch forward, the pain moved like a ball bearing in my head, and the aching, with which I was becoming familiar, suddenly flared again making me grimace. If the doctor noticed he said nothing. Unable to move I responded with words.

"Doctor you know nothing about me. The only reason that I'm stressed is that I've been let down by the man who was supposed to be my friend."

The spark of anger was the ignition for my body to move, and I managed to swing myself upright. I clambered to the end of the bed, clumsily reaching for my shoes. I put them on not bothering to tie my shoelaces. I picked up the suitcase and stumbled towards the door expecting the doctor to grab me, perhaps armed with a syringe to sedate me.

The doctor did not seem upset. He simply turned towards me and said calmly, "It might seem that way, Phil. I know my visit was unexpected. Perhaps you'd be more comfortable talking at the surgery. When you're ready you can make an appointment at the medical centre."

I left. I suspected the doctor must have been used to unstable characters behaving oddly, because as I turned to see his reaction I realised he had not looked up at my exit but was sitting writing up notes. I could hear the faint scratch of his fountain pen across the paper. Squiggly lines recording, for ever, my strange behaviour.

Chapter 11

Like a failed runaway I returned to my flat. The tartan suitcase bumped along behind me, my untied shoes clumping across the cobbles. The church bells were mocking me with their chimes. Their jubilation aggravated me. I should have been celebrating; after all I had done what I set out to do. I had resurrected a ghost. I was the hero.

But I had not been believed. Mac thought I was ill, Mac who had given me the idea initially; his interest had merely been a hoax. The clanging bells jarred against the hum in my head at the injustice of it.

Emma's eyes looked out from a poster, critically. 'You are mad,' she seemed to agree, in the disparaging way only a teenager can.

I crawled back to the bed in my room. It smelt damp. The familiarity of it was almost comforting. Falling into a restless sleep, I dreamt of hammers striking my head.

Waking later to a smear of sunshine outside, I lay for a time and watched the scudding clouds. After a while I realised the peace I felt was due, in part, to my head not banging.

I was not mad. With the clarity of my mind restored I was convinced I had seen the ghost of Mary Queen of Scots. Others did not have to believe me.

I had seen her. Instantly I felt brighter. The surge of success came back to me.

Now that I had seen Mary, there was no doubt I could do the same again. I would take the experiment to Ashton Wood on the fourteenth of February. I would see Laura again.

I managed to have a shower and put on some clean clothes, leaving the others rumpled on the floor. The flat was so untidy it made little difference.

I had to do something. My thoughts turned to Laura again and her friend, Kelly.

Grabbing my jacket I headed to the other side of town. The market square was busy with morning shoppers doing their chores. People and cars going to and from the supermarket.

The police incident unit was still stationed there adding to the congestion. I walked past it all keeping my head down.

The streets around Kelly's house were quieter, everybody out at work or school. Kelly's house was as silent as when I had previously visited. I knocked on the door, not holding out much hope of a reply. I held my finger on the bell so it played its tune over and over.

Nobody came. I started to turn away.

There was a sudden crunch on the gravel behind me and I jumped. The small woman standing there said, "Sorry. Didn't mean to startle you," and she smiled.

Her small, bulky frame was bustled into a beige raincoat tied sack-like with a belt. She was loaded down with two bulging carrier bags which made her look even shorter. To balance she had placed her feet wide apart so she appeared broader too, her thick ankles visible above her sensible lace up shoes, immoveable. She had a pleasant face though and a thick-lipped mouth, which continued to smile at me.

After a moment she frowned and asked, "It's Mr. Lockley, isn't it? Laura's dad. I was so sorry about all of that, so sorry my dear. It must have been a while ago, but the pain doesn't go away does it? Kelly is still upset by it. I think it's made her ill sometimes, them being such close buddies and all."

I'm sure Mrs. Johnson would have kept on talking, as if her heavy bags were anchoring her to the spot, if I had not intervened.

"When might Kelly be in? I need to speak to her."

"Oh." She seemed confused; I wondered whether she did not like the idea of Kelly talking to me.

"But Kelly should be in," she said. "She's not been well. Perhaps she's asleep and didn't hear you." I thought it unlikely with the length of time I had pressed the bell.

Mrs. Johnson finally lunged forward making me jump out of the doorway. Somehow she managed to retrieve her keys from her baggage and pushed open the door.

"Come in, come in." She called over her shoulder at me as she lumbered down the hallway to her kitchen. I waited by the door.

She returned quickly, removing her coat and revealing a dull purple outfit. She moved through the hall, her dumpy figure moving surprisingly swiftly and she bustled up the stairs, like a fat, fussing pigeon, the rustling of undergarments audible.

"Kelly. Kelly, love," she cooed as she vanished into the dim shadow of the landing.

Muttering and murmuring seemed to filter down but I couldn't make out any words. An upstairs door shut and Mrs. Johnson's small, sensibly clad feet appeared on the stairs.

"Teenagers," she tutted. "She's on the computer. These youngsters and computers. You know what it's like," she said thoughtlessly, forgetting I no longer had a child to grumble about. But she didn't seem to notice my discomfort and continued without taking a breath. "You can go up if you like. The study's the door facing at the top of the stairs."

I climbed the stairs with hesitation. Remembering the mousy, timid girl that had been Laura's friend, I didn't know what I would say. The small landing gave off to five doors. All were closed except the one to the right. Through the gap I could see the reflection of pink painted walls brightening the dull room. I presumed that was Kelly's bedroom.

I tapped lightly on the door ahead which I thought should be the study. There was a faint murmur of "Come in."

I opened the door onto a box room. As I did so Kelly quickly typed something on the computer keyboard and switched it off, so letters kept whirling across the blackened screen. The room was tiny. The shelves were piled with magazines, toy boxes and puzzles, as if this was the room where everything was tossed when it had outlived its usefulness.

There was not enough room for me to go in and shut the door, the space being taken up not only by a desk and computer, but mainly by the large girl sitting staring suspiciously at me. Kelly had blown up to at least twice the size she had been when I had last seen her. To call it puppy fat would have been kind but also a lie. I was taken aback.

"Hello, Kelly," I said over-brightly, realising how patronising I sounded, close to blurting out how much she'd grown. Even though she had gained weight there was a pretty quality about her. Her mousy hair was much blonder, probably dyed, and curled into ringlets. She was also wearing make-up so that her small blue eyes and rose bud mouth were emphasised. I was reminded of a baby doll Laura had been given as a young girl. The same smooth skin, overly blue eyes and red mouth.

"What do you want?" she demanded her lips moving into an obstinate pout.

"Can I ask you about Laura?"

"What?" she said, surprised, her face creasing up so that her eyes disappeared into her fleshy face. I was aware of the stuffy quality of the small room. The smell of hormonally charged sweat mingling with cheap perfume tainted the air. It wasn't surprising that Kelly became ill if she sat at the computer all day breathing this fug, I thought.

"I need to know if Laura was contacting somebody on the computer."

Kelly looked at me for a time as if weighing up what to tell me.

"Mm," she finally uttered, non-commitally. "What do you know?" she asked, revealing that there might be something to know.

"I don't know anything. That's why I've come here. Lately I've been thinking about Laura's death, it didn't seem quite right."

"Mm," she said again, her gaze moving over me continually as I stood awkwardly at the door. I realised Kelly would not give up any information on her own impetus, so I began to interrogate her, gently I hoped.

"Did she come here to use the computer?"

Kelly nodded slowly.

"Did she talk to friends?"

Kelly nodded again, a ringlet bouncing.

"And she met somebody?"

Again the head moved slowly, up and down.

"Who?" I shouted.

Kelly sat back in her chair suddenly looking frightened as if I might hit her.

"I don't know," she said unhappily.

"She talked to him on the computer, but did she really meet him?" I asked in a more friendly tone.

She nodded very slowly this time, so the hair stayed still. "I think so," she whispered.

"And you've no idea who this person was?"

This time the blonde head moved from side to side. "No."

"You've no idea at all. Can you remember the name? Or if this person was from round here?"

The negative head movement continued. "Everybody uses a different name on the computer. It could have been anybody."

The answer frustrated me and I wanted to grab Kelly and shake her into more action than the bobbing head movement. It would do no good though; Kelly had no reason to lie.

The grey computer box sat unconcerned on the floor, lights winking, the monitor smugly rotating its clever pattern of images, and I thought of the millions of people drawn to its innocuous space, using its blandness to deceive.

He could be anywhere. It was hopeless.

"Kelly, you cycled to Ashton Wood with Laura after school that day?" The question triggered a guilty expression on Kelly's face. She looked away from me and fixed her sight on the door frame. It made me consider that Kelly might know more than she was letting on, after all. "You did go with her, didn't you?"

Kelly said nothing her stony countenance unchanging. I suspected she had not been there at all. She had allowed her friend to walk alone into a trap. Looking at her resolute pout I didn't think she would confess to me.

"Did you say anything to the police?"

The idea shocked her into life again.. "No. It was an accident wasn't it?"

Of course, Kelly hadn't said anything to the police. At that time she was still a naïve, mousy little girl. Why would she think Laura's internet conversations were relevant to her death? Even if she knew Laura had been meeting somebody she had probably been bound by some secret teenage pact never to say anything. And so Laura's death had always been considered a tragic accident. The police weren't looking for paedophiles or conspiracies. She had been knocked off her bicycle by a car. And had died. The case was closed.

I made my way down the stairs, feeling more ancient and hunched than ever. If I thought Kelly had altered she probably had taken in my changed appearance. I used to think I was a trendy kind of father. Now I was shrivelled and old, in the same tatty clothes. Did I even still qualify as a father now I had no living offspring? The hollowness within me was suddenly conspicuous and expanded uncomfortably with the oppressive air of Kelly's study. I needed to leave.

At the bottom of the stairs Mrs. Johnson greeted me with a smile. "Would you like a cup of tea? I've just put the kettle on. Was Kelly alright? She's a good girl really. Such tragic times we live in."

She was blocking the stairs so I couldn't say a polite good bye and leave. My head was hammering again. What would I do now? What could I do, knowing that Laura's death might not have been as accidental as everybody had thought?

Mrs. Johnson was still guarding the bottom of the stairs as if she wasn't going to let me leave. A stream of would-be gossip came from her which she was determined I would reciprocate. I could see daylight through the glass panel in the front door, and wondered if I could just push pass her and escape, my desperation to breathe fresh air suddenly overwhelming.

"And now this awful disappearance. Such a lovely girl. Such a sweet girl. Used to come here a lot. A bit younger than Kelly but so mature for her age and so helpful. She'd always make me a nice cup of tea when I came in. Lovely manners."

She shook her head sadly, the grey curls bouncing, and I saw the resemblance between mother and daughter.

"Is this Emma Sutton, you're talking about? She used to come here?" I asked, the words Mrs. Johnson had spoken filtering into my fogged brain.

"Yes. They're so good with computers now aren't they, even the girls," she said with admiration in her voice. "Now, how about that cuppa?"

Finally she shifted into the hallway, so I could get by. I almost ran to the front door.

"No thank you, Mrs. Johnson."

I stumbled out, not looking back at her, into the fresh air feeling starved of oxygen.

At the gate I leant down supporting myself with my hands on my thighs. I took several deep breaths as if I had been about to faint. The cheap perfume still clung to my jacket. Gradually I straightened up.

A familiar black car was parked over the road. I pulled up my jacket collar and tried to dismiss the edgy sensation it gave me.

I walked unsteadily back into town. The weight of a possible connection between Laura and Emma thudded through my head, like a ball bearing in a game of pinball. I began to piece together D.I. Russell's inferences. It seemed to intensify my confusion.

I headed for Marti's shop, but the closed sign was there. Thursday was early closing and the shop was cold and quiet. I was disappointed. I needed somebody to talk to. Again I felt the hollow ache of being friendless.

My flat didn't help. The stale odour reached me as soon as I opened the door. It mingled with the strange scent of the damp bark I had collected. Just as I went to close the door, Ratty meowed and followed me in through the narrow gap.

"Hi, friend," I said, relieved that I didn't repel every living thing.

Dusk was falling. Usually I would have eventually made my way to the Talbot Hotel and downed a few pints. I could have pretended it would have lifted my mood. I did not want to speak to Mac though. Ever. He had betrayed me once too often. I prepared for a miserable night in with time to contemplate what Kelly's answers had hinted at, and also the fact that Emma Sutton had been a visitor there as well.

I made Ratty and me something to eat. Ratty was the one in ten of cats that was not particularly fussy about her diet.

Gradually, as my stomach filled with beans and toast, I felt calmer. Ratty finished her meal and I was certain I heard a noise that could have been a purr as she turned circles and settled on the hard kitchen chair.

The knocking on the door made us both start up from our seats. I knew it was trouble from the aggressive rap. It demanded to be answered. The person outside did not intend to go away.

As I got up I was aware of a flashing beacon outside which cast shadowy blue figures across the ceiling. A police car.

The knocking came again. Louder now, more impatient.

I got to the door just as the noise started again and a voice shouted, "Mr.Lockley….." I did not let them finish.

A female police officer was at the door. "Mr. Lockley?"

I nodded. Behind her I was aware of another dark shape hovering.

"May we come in a moment?"

I nodded again. Ratty took her opportunity to escape and I felt envy as she vanished into the evening.

The police officer stepped into the flat first, followed by D.I Russell. I pressed myself back against the wall trying to keep distance between us, but he still had to squeeze past me in the narrow passage, his sickly after shave once again overpowering every other sense.

They took their places in the kitchen. Unable to rewrite the script I sat on the chair opposite the detective. He looked around him in disdain at the mess. The unwashed crockery, the sieve still holding the bark pieces. I wished I had tidied up. His gaze eventually fell on the equipment in front of him. He looked at it for some minutes, saying nothing. Then, still looking at the machine, tipping his head from side to side trying to work out what it was, he asked, "Where were you today between one and two o'clock?"

"I went to see Kelly Johnson." So it had been them spying on me.

"So you're not denying you went to her house?"

"No. Why? What's happened?"

I was bewildered. Kelly had been perfectly alright when I had left. Perhaps Mrs. Johnson, beneath her friendly exterior, was actually worried I had upset Kelly. Perhaps Kelly had accused me of something, even though the door had remained open and Mrs. Johnson had no doubt been eavesdropping at the bottom of the stairs. My mind scrolled through hundreds of possibilities, none of them making any sense.

"Mr.Lockley, I am arresting you on suspicion of being implicated in the disappearance of Emma Sutton. You do not have to say anything. But it may harm your defence if you do not mention when questioned something that you later rely on in court. Anything you do say may be given in evidence. Do you understand?"

"No," I shouted. "No!"

I had never heard the Miranda phrase addressed directly to me. The words were as familiar as a well-known nursery rhyme. Its familiarity gave no comfort.

"I would like you to accompany us to the police station. It would be easier for all concerned if you did not make this any more uncomfortable for yourself than necessary."

The young police officer moved and I could see the glint of handcuffs behind her. I decided a confrontation would not be in my best interests. I would have to go with them quietly. Once we were away from my flat I could explain. Surely there had to have been a misunderstanding?

D. I. Russell grabbed my arm unnecessarily roughly considering my newly cooperative state. "Your flat will be searched," he said matter-of-factly. And then over my head to the officer he added, "Barton, make sure that machine is bagged up. I want it sent to the lab for analysis."

"Yes, sir."

I wanted to shout they couldn't take it. It was too important. I needed it to find Laura. But I knew no matter what I said they would remove it. Leaving the flat I felt bereft.

My feet made a hollow sound as they descended the metal steps to the yard. We had to exit the flat through the back yard and by the time we'd got round to the front, with the police light flashing, quite a crowd had been attracted. A few pedestrians hovered on the side walk, heads bobbing to see who was in trouble. Faces stared out from the café window; I could see people trying to stand up to get a better view. In less desperate circumstances I might have remarked they'd be better off watching the telly. I did not feel like joking.

Morelli's nephew was leaning against the café wall beyond the windows, in the shadows. At first I thought he was holding his phone in his hands because it glinted as it caught the blue strobe of light. But as I past him I realised it was the flash of a pen-knife blade. It was too dark to be sure if the youth was smiling but I had the sensation, even though his attention was on the implement, that he was watching me from under his long concealing eyelashes. I wanted to strike out at somebody; if he had been closer I would happily have punched him.

Barton pushed my head down as I bent into the back of the police car and was driven away. I presumed I was heading for the police station in Peterborough.

Chapter 12

The suburbs of Peterborough were familiar to me as we drove towards the city centre. Once upon a time, in my former existence as a journalist, I had prowled around the law courts, next door to the police station, waiting for stories. This was a different experience.

I had been inside Peterborough Police station before. In my student days occasionally a police officer would come in to the student digs late at night and ask for volunteers for a line-up. It had been a joke. We'd giggle and laugh our way through it unconcerned about crimes committed. It had been worth it for the novelty of a change to our routine and a couple of quid extra drinking money.

Nobody was unkind to me but I felt battered and brutalised by the time I was sitting in a cold cell. The harsh echoing air of the police station jarred me, as if the atmosphere had been tripped with invisible razor blades. My belongings were handed over and my pockets rifled through. It felt as if layers of me were being stripped away, leaving me raw with every nerve ending exposed and without anybody having even touched me.

Every movement clanged around the building. I could hear exaggerated noises of shouts and cell doors. Even pacing the cell, my loosened shoes clunking against the stone, seemed designed to unsettle me. The smell was overpowering as well. There was a stench of sweat mingled with bleach that combined to create a vile crescendo which accosted the nostrils. They had taken my jacket away so I had no comfort from its familiar odour. I sat on the edge of the uninviting pallet and stared at the rough white wall ahead of me, with its disturbing stains and graffiti. It reminded me that hundreds of other people had been here. Guilty or innocent I could feel their stain in the atmosphere hanging like an oppressive cloud of germs. Unclean and unseen.

Gradually my legs hunched up closer and closer to my body as if they were not controlled by me but by some animal instinct that instructed me to curl up into a small protective ball.

I wondered how long they would keep me here. I had no knowledge of the law. I had no idea even of the length of time they could leave me here. The more time I was away, the more interruption there was to my experiment. My skin felt taut as if I was being pulled further away from my goal of finding Laura.

I was an innocent man. Innocent until proven guilty, that's what the law said. So how would they prove my guilt if I was innocent? A vision of D.I. Russell's smug face sickened my thoughts, and physically I could feel bile rising in my throat. The certainty that he could prove whatever he wanted made my hands clammy. I wiped them on my jeans trying to remove the grimy sensation that clung to me. Recalling those days as a student in the identity parade gave me an odd sensation. I thought they hadn't affected me, but I knew with certainty whatever the circumstances, I had always been picked out of the line as the perpetrator, even though it was known I could not have been involved. The sensation of unspecified guilt came back to me multiplied with the passage of time.

At some point a tray of food was pushed into the cell. The food did not look appetising but I wouldn't have been able to taste it anyway. The inside of my mouth felt desensitised, as if my taste buds had been removed along with my possessions.

I had been told that the duty solicitor would visit me. It was made clear that it was unlikely that he'd make an appearance before morning. I suspected D.I. Russell had made an especial point of arresting me late in the day so I'd have a night in the cells. I wouldn't be able to prove this calculation but it made me a little more sympathetic to the people who believe we live in a police state.

The only way to deal with bullies like Russell was not to be phased by them. He wanted me to be cowed and scared by him. I vowed I would not be; at least I would not show it. The terrible trauma of Laura's death had given me a protective coating that repelled certain sensations; D.I. Russell was just one of them.

So I sat on the shelf, my feet up. I did not want to lie down with my nostrils too close to the thin mattress, breathing in the excoriate of other men. I felt haunted by them, inexorably connected to their misery and condition. The awareness hung about me that terrible things had passed and the future also held dreadful things. That was history. And I was just another endless link in the chain.

I had a limited choice of actions. I did not want to sleep, I did not want to think too deeply about D.I. Russell or my current situation, so I looked at my hand. At least it was familiar. The lines were deep wheals across my palm. What the hell did they mean? Marti would have been able to tell me. Were they really paths of my life leading to this cell? And would it have helped me if I had known? Did that line crossing a line mean that Laura would die? Was it inevitable? And what if someone had told me? Would I really have wanted to know? Or would that knowledge have tainted our time together aware that every second was a countdown to the explosion of her death?

I did not want to think about Laura, I needed to consider something bland and lifeless. So I turned my attention to the wall. In a vague remembrance of a Zen meditation exercise I thought of the wall, and then the bricks and then each individual brick and then I tried not to consider the brick at all.

Firstly, think of the wall; man made, brick on brick, one brick linked to the other by a skim of cement and then painted with a thin film of white wash.

Then, think beyond the bricks to the atoms.

That's all everything was.

Everything whirring atoms, particles that flew around, connected merely by a range of inevitable bonding. Bonds which were so predictable they always occurred.

Just as the bricks had no resistance to being placed side by side, did I really have any choice about my thoughts and feelings?

In the end it didn't matter what fancy names you gave to the hormones and neurotransmitters that moved through the system; they were still just building blocks.

Bricks and cement covered by a skin.

Walls and ceiling and floor and me.

Suddenly, the room had a transparency as I imagined every atom and the space between. The walls were a haze, as if created by a single object spun around me causing a continuous ashy miasma I could almost see beyond. I imagined myself suspended inside Marti's crystal ball. I could feel the pressure of her warm hands around it. Not sure if I was awake, only aware of being on the brink, I felt as if I was balancing on the rim of a volcanic crater.

I awoke to the clatter of the door grate being pulled back and before I opened my eyes I armed myself with the thought I would not let D.I. Russell win. I would not be beaten into submission by him. And then I said a brief prayer, not for understanding or even freedom, but for a reliable solicitor.

Chapter 13

I realised just how much the gods must disapprove of me when I saw the wiry weasel of a man appointed me by the Crown. I regretted turning down the offer of choosing my own solicitor. Yesterday evening, when it had been suggested, I was in no position to make a decision. I had allowed the die to be cast, and lost.

The solicitor was probably a nice man at home with his family or friends, but here he just seemed insignificant. He was small and dark with a pinched up face and high voice. His suit appeared ragged at the cuffs but on closer inspection wasn't. It was just the way the material hung against his thin, hairy wrists. I wondered if he really was as strange as he appeared or whether it was a distorting effect the jail had on everything. If there was such an effect it seemed to elude D.I Russell. His clean hands, puffed up hair and shiny shoes seemed untouched by the taint. Perhaps the aftershave he wore had a certain enchanting ingredient; it certainly wrapped about him like a protective suit of armour.

The solicitor gave little advice. I felt more desolate with him beside me than I had been alone in the cell.

As we made our way down the corridor to the interview room, the cool air and white brickwork appeared solid and confining. The cold surfaces reflected all senses heightening the atmosphere with anxiety. The insipid figure of the solicitor, at least two inches shorter than me, did not inspire confidence.

Unlike the interview rooms in T.V. programmes, the room was quite light and airy. Narrow windows, striped with mesh, edged the top of the wall adjoining the corridor; I could see the flickering strip lights.

Whether it was simply a result of little sleep and an uncomfortable cell, my body felt limp and awkward. I couldn't decide how to sit; straight, which might give the impression of aggression, or laid back with my legs extended and arms open-palmed by my side, as if I didn't care. Neither position seemed appropriate nor could I control my limbs to an intermediate state. I switched between the two in an awkward, rebellious dance.

Opposite me D.I. Russell sat, cool and calm. His neatness mocked my dishevelled puppetry. We were like two sides of a coin; he the noble head on one side, me the scattered pattern on the other.

His aftershave gradually seeped into the air, making me aware of our occupying the same space and sharing the same oxygen.

He sat for several moments, quiet and confident, maintaining an easy manner, as if he was sitting in a restaurant waiting patiently for a meal he knew would soon arrive and satisfy his appetite. He had the same cruel turn of his lips that showed he was taking pleasure in my discomfort. I would not be eating.

He gave a small cough, just clearing his throat in anticipation.

Then he introduced the four people at the table, for the tape. This was a duel though, between the two of us, the other participants merely the cloak-holding seconds.

"So, Mr. Lockley," he drawled. "Let's make this simple shall we? Tell me what happened with Emma."

The sentence pulled me up into the straight aggressive pose. We could keep this simple, very simple; I could just hit his smirking face. My shoulders were on a mechanism wound by anger and I felt them rise tightly towards my ears. I expected my face was turning red, but I couldn't speak. The words twisted in my mouth and I gagged and spluttered.

"Get Mr. Lockley a drink of water," the D.I. requested pleasantly of a shadow in the corner of the room, who obeyed.

I sipped the water, and knew the detective was watching every nervous tic of each twisted sinew. He had definitely had the first blow.

A soup of thoughts whirled in my head. "Get a grip," I thought desperately. "You're innocent. Just tell him you're innocent."

Finally my mouth responded and the words fell with surprising confidence. "I had nothing to do with the disappearance of Emma Sutton. I did not know her."

"You were in the wood trying to delete her initials on the tree."

"No. I was just collecting bark." It sounded a strange thing to be doing, even to me, when the words were caught in the constricting air of the interview room. I was aware of the tense man beside me. I could sense the beads of perspiration oozing from his pale brow, every thought from him loaded with the notion, 'this man is mad.'

"But you were round at Kelly Johnson's house?"

"Yes."

"So you used Kelly's computer to talk to young girls like Emma."

"No, I don't have a computer, I don't use computers, and I've certainly never used Kelly's computer."

"What name do you use in the chat rooms?"

"I don't use chat rooms."

"And you pretend to be a young chap, with the same interests? You gain their trust and then you meet up."

"No."

"I expect Laura was a bit shocked to find you waiting for her rather than the handsome young man you'd pretended to be."

"No. No."

My head was in my hands. How could this so-called detective be constructing such a story? It was like a violent fairy tale. And beneath the accusations was the dreadful thought that Laura might have been sucked into this sort of dreadful game with an unknown person deceiving her and her friends, by a false promise of friendship and romance. I could hear their twittering giggles as Laura got ready to meet this computer 'friend'. Thankfully, Russell's distinct voice broke my thought trail.

"We know you're involved Mr. Lockley. We discovered Kelly erasing all her files when we interviewed her after your visit."

"I wouldn't know how to erase files."

"Kelly does. You went round there to instruct her to do it."

"No."

"She seemed pretty upset when we saw her."

"That wasn't my doing. She was fine when I left."

"Really? I'd say she was extremely agitated. Yes, if you'd stormed round there to make sure she destroyed evidence on her computer I think you would have been very intimidating."

"I didn't storm round anywhere. I asked her a few questions. I didn't upset her."

"Well, her mother thought you were acting strangely."

Perhaps if I'd stayed for that cup of tea Mrs. Johnson would have had a more benevolent view of me.

"We've got Kelly's computer at the moment. Our technical specialists are at this very moment analysing all its files. If there is anything on there, anything at all Mr.Lockley, we'll find it. Now, another thing." He did his photograph trick again, sliding a set of photographs onto the table. "Tell me about these."

I looked at them. Initially they made no sense. Just a muddy surface covered with some tracks or lines marked in the dirt.

I picked one up to have a closer look, frowning.

Shaking my head and shrugging I slid it back towards Russell. "No idea."

He pushed the photograph towards me again. "So you can't see the star?"

I leant down and looked. It did seem as if there was symmetry to the lines. The circle was the most obvious shape and then five smaller darker and raised areas that could have been the points of a star.

"I suppose it could be a star. What's it got to do with me?"

"Witchcraft, Mr. Lockley. Tell me about your little experiments. You make potions from oak trees. You pick the bark from them. You probably hug them." He paused, inhaling through his nose, a bull preparing to charge. "And you construct equipment capable of giving somebody an electric shock. Don't look so surprised Mr. Lockley. We know the machine we found in your flat was used for torture. It gives off quite a nasty electric shock."

It sounded as if I had been hiding the machine. But the question made it appear as if they had had to dissect the flat to discover it, not that it had been sitting on display on my kitchen table. If it had given Russell a shock I was glad. I looked at his fingers to see if I could see any blackened evidence of a scorch mark, but of course did not.

My mouth opened to refute it but no words came out.

"These markings were found quite near Ashton Wood, in the old mill buildings. Quite a celebration you had there, we think?"

"Not me. No."

"According to my sources there would have been quite a gathering last Wednesday.

Besides the pentagram, there would have been candles burning. Some interesting herbs were found, mushrooms and the like. Oh, and blood."

I was horrified. Was he going to indict me of being involved in every recent crime? Perhaps he would dig up the files of those line-ups I had done as a student and accuse me of those as well?

"This has nothing to do with me."

"Where were you on Wednesday?"

A horrible echo resonated from my gut to my head and I thought I might be sick. I heard Marti's warm voice saying sleepily, "If any one asks, tell them you were with me."
And my stupid thought being, 'Who would ask?' There was a horrible inevitability about it. And now I was meant to lie. Lie for Marti and dig myself deeper into this morass.
What could I say?

"So where were you?"

"I can't remember."

"You don't know where you were on the first of February. That was an important day for you this year, wasn't it Mr. Lockley?"

I didn't know what he was talking about. Only that Marti had been involved with pentagrams on the first of February and had pulled me in to her deceit.

"You surprise me Mr. Lockley. I would have thought any witch or wizard would be out on February the first."

"I'm not a wizard. I don't have anything to do with any of that."

But Marti did. I couldn't believe she was involved in black magic, but that was how it was appearing. Fury began to bubble below the surface of my skin and I knew my face was reddening. Russell leaned forward, aware of my discomfort but could not know the truth behind it. It just made me look guilty.

"So you weren't at the Imbolc feast?"

"No." My mind raced to recall anything about Imbolc. Was it a black magic festival? I could not remember.

"So tell me about your potions then, Mr. Lockley, and the intriguing machine."

I was going to have to tell him. I was going to have to tell him about the experiment. The heat of that thought burnt the back of my head and fought its way forward until I had to spit the words out, knowing I would be ridiculed and thought insane. But I had to tell him.

I tried to tell my story as straight forwardly as possible. To make it sound more rational. I started by saying that Mac had asked me to write an article about the Talbot Hotel and the haunting by Mary Queen of Scots. I then laughed in an attempt to lighten the atmosphere. It came out like a demented cackle. I explained I'd decided to take the article idea a bit further with the Kirlian device and my crazy experiment. I looked around in the hope of seeing a smile or softening of features, but only saw frowns.

I said nothing about Laura.

"So you're not into witchcraft Mr. Lockley, you're just a regular ghost buster." For the first time he turned to his colleague and they shared the joke. The traitor at my side managed a smile.

"What about going to the wood? You don't deny that?"

"No, I go there all the time. Just to walk or take photos."

"Interesting then that your blood was found on the tree where Emma carved her initials."

"What? But I was collecting bark. You saw me. I cut myself, that's all." I pushed my thumb forward like a blunt weapon, showing the torn dirty rip caused by the bark.

The man beside me winced, with an audible intake of breath, not with sympathy at the gash on my thumb, but at the audacity of the gesture.

D.I. Russell pushed back from the table as if he had been threatened, and I felt the solicitor beside me now shivering as if he might be preparing to run. I could sense him shrinking with each reply I gave, so I thought by the end of the interview I might turn and find only an oily patch where he had been.

Regaining his calm D.I. Russell said, "For the benefit of the tape, Mr. Lockley has shown me a gash on his thumb," sealing the threat as evidence for any future listener.

I looked around at my solicitor for what I hoped might be an encouraging nod but instead he sniffed and avoided eye contact. I wondered if he was on the side of D.I. Russell who thought I was mad. As the interview progressed the little man seemed to sidle further and further away from me as if concerned about contamination.

All I could tell them was my story.

In the end I suspected it was so far-fetched as to leave them no choice but to accept it.

D.I. Russell huddled with his colleague, whispering and nodding and shaking his head in a surreal dance. Finally Russell turned to me and said simply, "You're free to go."

I made to get up but he pushed across the table, moving so quickly I thought he was going to grab me. I sat down again and faced his mean-eyed stare. "We may need to talk to you again." He finished with a sarcastic hiss. "Take care, Mr.Lockley."

As we stood up the solicitor reached his hand out and smiled, as if we had just made an important business deal. He shook my hand. "Don't worry Mr. Lockley, we'll get this sorted." As if we were a team.

I grumbled a thank you. After all even if he was useless and thought me mad, I might still need him. A plea of insanity was always an option.

I wanted to run out, get away from that stinking building and horrible people but first I had to go and collect my things. I pulled on my jacket with relief but it didn't feel the same.

Chapter 14

I was greeted by a dull February sky, the colour and consistency of frothing, malicious spittle. The only means of transport available to me for my return to Oundle was my own feet or the bus. I did not have the energy to walk and the bus station was the other side of town.

For a while, I wandered round aimlessly, my thoughts churning. I couldn't decide what to do next. I really needed to get on with my experiment for Laura but didn't have the heart for it at the present. The gardens below the cathedral were dull with no signs of spring evident. I sat on a damp bench and watched the traffic queue at the roundabout spewing filthy fumes and noise. There were few people about. Those that walked through the park ignored me. My hair was dishevelled, the stubble on my face rough and greying. In my filthy jacket and tatty clothing I must have looked like a tramp.

A nauseous hunger spread through me, the sort of sensation that would have been satisfied with either alcohol or food. I thought I'd better stick to food. I bought a greasy bacon bap from a van as I made my way to the town centre. It remained a fatty undigested lump in the pit of my stomach.

For some reason, an image of Ratty came into my head and I wondered if she needed feeding. She had probably eaten; she was more capable of fending for herself than I was.

Slowly I ambled on through the town towards the bus station. I took a detour through the Cathedral Square to avoid the busy streets and I was drawn to go inside and see the place where Mary Queen of Scots had once been buried.

As I crossed the green in front of the cathedral, I heard the piping call of a child echo around the huge arches of the west front; I looked around but saw no one. The suggested solitude that the cathedral bestowed made my steps towards it more certain. The carved saints above the archway watched me with their placid gaze as I entered.

Immediately, as with entering most churches and cathedrals, I was aware of a tranquillity about the place making everybody bend into whispering piety. Even I, with my unwashed body and dirty clothing, was accepted.

The space was huge. It was amazing that great pillars of stone weighing tonnes to support the mass of the building above could have such delicacy. Even with the dullness of the day outside there was a gentle light illuminating the wan stone. Everything rose towards it. I walked slowly down the central aisle. Footsteps and quiet words from the few people present were audible like the repetition of prayer. It was a comforting background noise but I was not particularly aware of the other visitors. It was the shadows that murmured, intensifying even the smallest sound. They carried to the vaulted roof where they were then gently dispersed like doves released.

The pillars were beautiful, fanning up to the roof with dendritic sprays fingering upwards and outwards, outstretched hands supporting an earthly illustration of heaven. One ceiling was terracotta with gold ridges running through it in a geometric square which enclosed an eight pointed star. At each point was a rosette. I was reminded of the photograph of the ritual site D.I. Russell had shown me. How tied we were as a race to shapes and symbols. Stars and crosses and circles. Believing the patterns and symmetry of each could somehow reflect our own beliefs and shape our own destiny.

The nave ceiling work was patterned with a blue diamond design, each with a central painted motif. The artistry and architecture led the eye towards a predominant image. The rood cross suspended beneath the central tower. It was a modern piece, placing a skeletal Christ against a red cross. The tortured body was the same shade of ivory as yellowed teeth. It was bold in its portrayal of tormented suffering. With its modern simplicity it jarred bright against the background of the softer ancient tone of the cathedral. It was an image that would not be ignored. As I looked, with my neck craned back, it appeared to resonate with anguish.

For a while I knelt in one of the wooden choir stalls and imagined myself invisible. I could still see the suspended figure above me. Even when I averted my gaze I was aware of Him hanging there in his misery. Was suffering the thing that made us human? I never really did grasp religion, the fact that an all powerful being could actually stand by and let all the misery happen. How could a benevolent deity let Laura be taken away from me? Sometimes when terrible things occurred in other people's lives they actually turned to religion. To me it seemed sadistic. I remembered mother lying in bed, silent except for her breathing, a noisy rattle of tormented respiration. She had liked to listen to the daily church service. It did seem to soothe her. I think she enjoyed the calming, steady voice of the priest. I preferred the hymns. They were the uplifting part.

Mother always retained an element of religious belief and behaviour. When I was a young boy she would try to make me say my prayers each evening. I would kneel at the bottom of her bed and say the Lord's Prayer out loud. She would murmur along with me and then she would give me a few moments to add my own silent missives. I was always restless by then, aware of my bony, schoolboy knees becoming uncomfortable on the thin carpet. I couldn't concentrate my mind on the words or thoughts I wanted to express. Perhaps that was why my prayers were ignored.

It was too cool to sit for long so I continued to pace around the cathedral. Having become better acquainted with Mary Queen of Scots I was glad to see the Scottish flag present in remembrance of her first resting place. She didn't have quite the grand burial tomb of Katharine of Aragon, who rested behind ornate black grating embellished with gold lettering, stating her position as 'Katharine Queen of England.' Both women had really been no more than strangers in these parts but had not been entirely forgotten. Neither had the grave digger who had buried them. A portrait of 'Old Scarlett', leaning on his shovel, hung at the back of the cathedral.

I decided to make my way back home. As I left the shelter of the cathedral square it began to spit with rain. I moved quickly to the warmth and artificial light of the enclosed shopping centre. After the quiet of the cathedral the centre seemed even busier. Even so, the two places seemed to have a link both feted with some kind of religious fervour. Sickly displays of chocolates spilled behind glass with posies and ribbons. From the shop windows giant teddies of every colour and size, adorned with satin bows and hearts, awaited hugs, their tubby arms outstretched. I wished I had a reason to buy one. Laura would have loved them.

Every window display declared promises of cuddles and kisses and everlasting love. The centre was throbbing with people but all of them managed to avoid me. An open pathway made my passage easy as people side stepped from me. Even those with heavy bags swayed from my path. I suspected I not only looked disgusting but probably stank too.

I waited in the ashy grime of the bus station, feeling more in tune with those soiled surroundings. The various hangers-on for public transport loitered like jetsam discarded from the shopping centre. It started to rain more heavily, the drops coalescing and running down the plastic shelter in dirty rivulets.

There was no desperation for me to get home but I felt frustrated by the waiting. A few people clambered aboard when the bus arrived but it seemed as though I had it to myself. The other users sat at the front in a little group leaving me in my own stench at the back of the coach.

I didn't care. I would have escaped from myself if I could.

The journey seemed longer than usual and by the time we arrived in Oundle market square the daylight had gone.

I had decided to go straight to the flat and sleep and try to shut out the horrible night just past. The rain was heavier now bestowing the stone and pavements with a benevolent sheen. Again I was aware of the shop windows crammed full of Valentine delights. The shops around the market square were still active and as the bus pulled passed I could see the door to Marti's shop open and a customer coming out. A sudden burn of anger flared up and my decision changed. I would see Marti.

That's where I would go.

I slammed through the door. The pathetic tinkle of the door chime ridiculed my angry posturing. Marti looked up from the service counter with a ready smile that quickly faded.

"Why don't you go through to the back Phil," she said smoothly. There appeared to be no undercurrent of fear or guilt as she said it, just a desire to soothe my obvious agitation. I felt my anger increase but did as she asked.

Marti talked quietly to the customers in the shop then I head the door chime and the lock being put on the door.

I was standing, pacing about the small back room in almost darkness.

"Let's have some light, shall we?" Marti continued, picking up a taper to light the candles. But I couldn't control myself anymore. I grabbed out and held her arm tightly.

"Ow! You're hurting me Philip," Marti said trying to wriggle from my hold and for the first time I saw a flicker of fear in her eyes. I liked the sensation. For once somebody had to listen to me. I held tighter.

"You hurt me! You set me up! The bruises aren't physical but they're there just the same."

"Philip. Philip," she repeated my name again, more loudly as if she was worried I wouldn't hear. "Philip, I don't know what I've done. Let me go and we can talk."

Perhaps it was the repetition of my name that affected me, but suddenly I felt totally exhausted and the shame of hurting her washed over me. I despised men who were violent to women, but for a moment I had enjoyed the sense of power it gave me. Feeling utterly drained I sat down, folding my arms on the table. I hunched my head into them and sobbed.

When I looked up the candles had been lit, their image a multi-faceted effect reflected through my tears.

The kettle was boiling and Marti made tea, straightforward brown tea with milk this time. She put a plate of bread and cheese in front of me. Before either of us spoke I ate every thing and drank the tea. Once I had finished I pushed the plate and cup away from me as if clearing the space ready for our exchange.

As if on cue, Marti came and sat down opposite me.

"The police questioned me."

Marti nodded.

"They asked where I was on Wednesday the first." I watched her but she didn't show any flicker of understanding, and I couldn't work out what she was thinking. Briefly, I wondered whether she had predicted it all, which is why she had asked for such a peculiar alibi. "That's the night you asked me to lie about where you were."

Marti nodded. Her coolness riled me. I raised my voice.

"When you're facing D.I. Russell across the interview desk, under arrest, after a sleepless night in the cells, you do not want to make the situation worse. You do not need to know that your so-called friends have dropped you in it, have got the police thinking that you're involved in witchcraft. What the hell have you been doing Marti?"

I did not mean to but I leant across the table viciously shouting the last words. I was reminded of D.I. Russell doing the same thing to me and I slunk back in my chair, a warm flush of shame creeping colour into my face again. Events were transforming me into a person I did not recognise and I did not have the capacity to halt it.

Marti screwed up her eyes and fists and took a deep breath. Then opening her eyes and spreading her fingers calmly on the table she began to apologise.

"I'm sorry. Sometimes things take an unexpected turn. I didn't mean you to get into trouble."

"I manage to cope with trouble when it comes from D.I. Russell. What worries me is how you are involved with this magic stuff. They showed me photos. I saw what you'd been doing."

I could see the images in my head, the ashy remains of dead things, the suggestion of blood and sacrifice, the pentagram, the symbol of their black rituals. "What the hell are you involved in?"

"It's not what you think. People just don't understand. That's why it's kept quiet."

"But it was alright to involve me, was it?"

"No. It wasn't right. But it happened."

"Tell me what really went on then. What is Imbolc? Who did you sacrifice?"

Marti lifted her head up and laughed. It was a pleasant laugh, not a witch's cackle, and I felt relieved.

"Philip, you don't really think that we'd sacrifice a human? If the police had found human remains there, you don't think they'd have let you go if they thought you'd been involved?"

"No," I said feeling stupid.

"Look, it's an important festival. But it's not black witchcraft. We're not evil. It's a neopagan celebration."

I must have looked bewildered. She began to explain.

"The word Imbolc comes from the Gaelic for ewes milk. This is the time of the first lambs. The feast is a welcoming of the Spring, a time of growth and renewal. Other religions have festivals. For Christians it's their Candlemas now. The light from the winter darkness."

She paused and looked up at me, checking to see if my mood was lightening. I did not flinch.

"The old mill is a good place. Besides being isolated there's still some old agricultural equipment from when it was a museum. We use those in the rites and bless the plough. Again it's just to do with the onset of spring. Something humans have been celebrating since the dawn of time."

"So why the blood?"

At the mention of blood she looked quite excited and leant towards me across the table. I duly leant back.

"Well this year, one of the farmer's actually did have a lamb born, just a few days before. It doesn't often happen. He thought it was a really good sign. He kept the placenta; we blessed it and burned it. It's a truly wonderful omen."

She realised I did not appear convinced.

"So it's mad. But only as mad as you, dear Philip, and your ghosts."

She managed to reach one of my hands which were tightly folded across my chest. Again the warmth of her hand seemed to resurrect my fingers into human entities capable of movement and my rage subsided. She kept hold of my hand squeezing it reassuringly.

"What about the missing girl, Emma Sutton. Was she involved?"

"No. Children aren't invited to the night celebration. They'd be lighting candles at home and planting seeds. I don't think the Sutton family are part of our coven either. I don't think any of her close family is involved." She paused, pressing my hand more firmly.

"Look Philip, people are pretty predictable, they like to have rituals and beliefs. We humans need to know that after the winter the spring will arrive. It doesn't matter which religion you follow, we all have our rites of spring. It keeps us hanging on. Otherwise most people would probably just give up." She smiled at me and I felt my mouth try and move into a reciprocal expression.

"Why don't you stay?"

I was tempted but still felt soiled from my incarceration.

"I can't," I said simply. Marti released my hand and I gradually pulled my fingers from hers. They moved with some reluctance, which seemed to emanate from my hand, not from the instruction given by my brain. Finally, it allowed me to go. I stood up and left.

Chapter 15

I expect hibernating animals must feel disorientated when they wake, just as I did the following morning. I awoke still in the clothes from the previous day. There was an empty bottle beside the bed; I vaguely remembered drinking myself into a stuporous sleep. I was coiled, aching all over and aware of my own stench. I was foul and soiled. Not just my clothes but my skin, my body, even the residual air in my lungs. Grit from sleep clogged my eyes and blurred my vision, but not enough to conceal the wretched panorama about me. As my nostrils began to absorb the odour of rotting wood and decay mingling with my own sweat, I knew the time had come to clear up. My head hurt. Looking around it felt worse. 'Spring Cleaning' my mother-in-law would have said with a cheery voice. As if the chores were a joy, proof that cleanliness was next to godliness. I was far removed from either. I started to move.

In the kitchen I found a bin bag at the back of a cupboard and began throwing debris into it. I started slowly but as the bag filled I became fired up and moved more quickly and threw things in with increased vigour. I piled books up and put them on the shelves I had wiped clean.

Once the flat was refreshed and tidy I focused on my own cleanliness. Restricted by the dribble of shower, I still managed to lather myself with soap and rinse every inch of my hair and skin. For once I shaved, the pull of the blade across my face a pleasant exfoliation. If I could have I would have stripped down to the bone and regenerated a completely new epidermis. Pink with scrubbing I picked up all the clothing on the floor, bundled it into the sheets from my bed, and changed into a grotty but clean tracksuit.

Launderettes are usually pleasant anonymous places, everybody intent on cleaning their dirty laundry privately.

Often it's the same folk who are there so a cursory nod of greeting is exchanged. Today was different. Old Charlie was reading his paper but instead of looking over the top and giving the usual acknowledgement he looked down, covering his face with the paper before I had time to make eye contact. I put all my washing in to one of the big machines, even my beloved jacket, and as the company seemed hostile I decided to take a stroll whilst waiting. I left the fuggy, soap-smelling warmth and headed into the cold day.

In the street people I'd have expected a "Morning" or smile from avoided me. One young woman holding a child by the hand, actually crossed the road rather than pass by me on the narrow pavement. I realised with shock I was no longer the anonymous man in the green jacket. I was a household name muttered about in the same appalled chunterings as child molesters and murderers. I felt people shy away from me as I walked across the square. A turn of the shoulders, a closing of curtains and the papery eyes of Emma Sutton still fixing me with their accusing glare.

I kept my head down and made for the clanging sounds coming from the direction of the Talbot Hotel. My head still felt uncomfortable but I wanted to get away from the warm soap and soporific throb of the launderette and felt I might at least be welcomed at the Talbot. I was half right.

Outside the front of the Hotel was a large truck delivering beer barrels. They were rolled to the side of the truck and then there would be a yell and the metal barrel was dropped onto a cushioned pad onto the front yard. The cushion had little effect in reducing the ringing thud as the cask struck the ground. Jamie was there, shouting instructions to an unseen body in the truck. He had a clipboard and pen in his hand. Another barrel had just landed near his feet when he looked up at me.

Initially I thought he was going to ignore me like everybody else, but then, "Hey, Phil. Did na recognise you without that jacket."

"It's in the wash. I had a bit of a run in with the police."

"Ai, I heard."

Oundle was not a large enough town for trouble to go unnoticed.

"I canna stop. Got ta get these barrels in."

Another man, clad in overalls marked with a beer company logo, appeared and was moving the barrels into a row beside the trap door which opened to the cellars below.

Jamie nodded up at the figure on the lorry as another barrel toppled out. He checked the clip board and marked the paper.

The operation looked to be going quite smoothly but I still wanted to be useful. "Do you want a hand?" I thought Jamie hesitated momentarily, as though he might just say yes. But he shook his head.

"Na, yer aw'right. Health and safety an all that. Cheers though." His attention returned to his clip board. I watched from a distance. One man disappeared below into the cellar, the other delivery man jumped down from the back of the truck and moved over to the cellar door cover shouting down, "Ready, Mick?"

Mick obviously was because the barrels started to be rolled down into the unseen space beneath ground. After they had all disappeared there was another shout and the process was reversed. Barrels appeared from the hole and were lined up on the side of the path. They made a different sound and were moved more quickly so were obviously the empties. It would be nice to have a straightforward job. Counting out full casks and collecting empty ones. It seemed refreshing in its simplicity.

There seemed no point in hanging around here. I made my way back to the launderette. Old Charlie had gone and though most of the machines were running nobody else was waiting. I sat and picked up Old Charlie's discarded paper and awaited my clean laundry, the tossing of water within machines a suitable accompaniment to my hangover.

Warm clothing emerged an hour later and I folded it and put it in bags. Happily I restored my jacket onto my person and ambled across the square. Again I felt eyes regarding me suspiciously as though I might abduct somebody right there.

Morelli's nephew was sitting astride his motorbike, holding court near the café surrounded by a few mates. He didn't have the operatic gesticulations of his uncle but he did have a dramatic posturing that was keeping his friends amused. He had obviously seen me and I knew I had become the topic of conversation from the whispering and surreptitious glances my way. He didn't look directly at me but a couple of the others turned their heads and stared. A skinny girl who was probably no more than thirteen or fourteen but dressed to appear older scowled at me with a hateful intensity as though I'd done her a personal wrong. Perhaps she had been at school with Emma and thought I was responsible. She was heavily made-up and with clothing that revealed a lot of skin and leg. Her reproachable stare followed me as I crossed the square but her jutting hips were directed pointedly towards the boy on the bike, her body leaning crudely towards him as he whispered something to the group in an exaggerated manner. She moved her stick legs into a new pose, still with her pelvis set fixedly, as if she were a mannequin in a suggestive window display.

I was glad to be back inside. Blessed with the sensation of cleanliness and of having achieved something. I would have celebrated with a meal for two, me and Ratty sharing a tin of tuna, but my companion was nowhere to be seen. I turned on the radio and listened to an afternoon play.

Chapter 16

The spring clean had had a beneficial effect on me, but I still awoke the next morning with a feeling of agitation. It was only two days until I needed to perform the second experiment. Laura's experiment. My Kirlian device was sitting somewhere, stored as some kind of evidence. Ready to be used against me. The problem was it was Sunday. Paddy's would be closed and I knew I would not be able to find that kind of store open around here on a Sunday. The church bells started ringing out and I wondered whether it would help to spend some time immersed in worship. I felt restless and needed something to occupy me.

I left the bells to peal out their familiar summons to folk more redeemable than me, grabbed my jacket and headed out into the dull morning. With the momentum of spring cleaning the flat yesterday I decided to head for the studio and potter about there. Whether it was my restless mood or a premonition the house itself seemed unsettled as if constricted by the low clouds. I crept in desperate not to attract Sarah's attention.

As I approached the studio I could tell something was not right. The door didn't appear to be locked. I slowed and listened for any indication that somebody was in there. Not a sound. Carefully I pulled the door open wide.

At first nothing seemed out of place, but the atmosphere was unsettled as if the dust had been shifted around. I was right; I could see a circle of clean table where the lamp base had not been replaced exactly. A snake of flex was trailing from the doors below the bench seat. The little piece of curled paper on the cork board had fallen and the board tilted at an angle disclosing a line of grime.

The usual state of the studio was ordered chaos. The chaos remained but in a different combination. I felt my teeth clench together and my fists coil as I realised some stranger had been here. Anger made me tense as I imagined them pulling open the drawers and cupboards, rooting through the files of photographs. In disturbing my things they had troubled me. My senses felt rifled.

I collapsed into the armchair as if I had been deflated and was incapable of standing any longer. Nothing seemed to have been taken, the most expensive pieces of equipment still in their places. So who?

The police. It must have been the police. They had been here. Touching everything. Leafing through my life.

I wondered why Sarah hadn't mentioned it. An alarm of some kind would have been nice. But it would have made little difference. They'd still have come in with their heavy boots and latex covered fingers. Sorting and sifting and inevitably finding nothing. It would have been worth it to see the disappointment on D.I Russell's face when he couldn't find any pornographic or paedophile prints.

The impetus for cleaning had gone. I left the studio, kicking the door shut and locking it again. As I turned I caught a glimpse of the kitchen net curtain move. I must have disturbed Sarah after all. But it wasn't Sarah's silhouette at the window. The shape had been wrong. Not small but big. Not a woman but a man. Mac. My god! Mac was here. Mac visiting early on a Sunday morning. No wonder she had been too busy to let me know about the police visit.

As I marched across the soggy lawn I wondered if I had been mistaken. I could no longer see the hulking apparition I thought was Mac. Still, I could not stop my momentum now my strides had lengthened with indignation. I rapped on the back door until it was opened. Anger made me taut and it took time for me to unclench my jaw to speak, giving Sarah the opportunity to start a torrent of apology. "Philip. I'm so sorry. You've seen the shed then? I'm sorry, I couldn't stop them. They searched the house too. I am really sorry."

It was difficult to maintain my ire in the face of such contrition. Her face looked pinched and I knew it must have been hard for her. She obviously thought my angry demeanour was just because the police had wrecked my studio. I wanted to shake her and tell her the idea of her and Mac together hurt me more but I couldn't find the words. Unable to release these emotions, my frustration increased.

"Sarah, is everything aw' right?" came Mac's call from the hallway. He pushed open the kitchen door and hesitated as he saw me. I thought I might implode with pent up rage and the humiliation of the situation.

"Philip's just found out that the police have searched the shed."

That's not all I had found out. I knew which made me feel worse.

I stepped into the kitchen, onto the white tiles, in my muddy boots and felt a bolt of satisfaction. Sarah recoiled as if she had been slapped. The intensity of my anger seemed to reduce with the action. I was acting like a child who has stamped his foot so hard that the pain triggered by the action, coursing up his leg, has momentarily taken his mind off the cause he is fighting.

Mac was still loitering at the door. Like a trapped beast he was unsure whether to advance or retreat, knowing he was captured either way.

"Look, I'm tha' sorry," he said. I wasn't sure whether he was commiserating with my break-in or apologising because I had found him co-habiting with my ex-wife. Either way he appeared genuinely upset.

I looked at them both; Mac awkward in the doorway, Sarah still distressed due to the police visit, stilted in front of me, wanting to clean the mess I had made on her pristine kitchen floor. If I stayed with their remorse as bright as the kitchen appliances I would forgive them too easily.

For several moments we looked at each other in the silence of the clean white space. The absence of noise was so complete it created an echo. The glossy units and surfaces seemed to reflect our thoughts into a virtual telepathic conversation. Nobody moved. Finally I gave in.

"It doesn't matter. They didn't break anything or take anything. It's about time I sorted it out anyway." I turned away, knowing my feeble gesturing had come to nothing. Sarah would put on her Marigolds and quickly wipe the muddy footprints up and then my tantrum would be forgotten.

I abandoned the studio, the house, Mac and Sarah, and started walking. Without much thought I turned away from my usual route down to Ashton Wood. I was keeping that unblemished for my Tuesday night rendezvous. Today I would head for Fotheringhay.

It was about a seven mile round trip across country. The distance did not concern me. I was used to walking. Glad to leave the wreckage of the studio and thoughts of Mac and Sarah behind, I began to enjoy the stretch of freedom in my legs, remembering all too keenly the confinement of the prison cell.

Once I was away from the town, my back firmly set against my problems, I started to relax. It was a cold dull day with a grim sky. It would probably rain.

The even rhythm of my steps was soothing and my anger at Sarah and Mac began to dissipate. Though they didn't seem to realise the hurt it produced to see them together, I knew they actually cared about me. Without them I was friendless. I could not consider such a solitary existence. Somehow I would have to accept their relationship. I concentrated on the benefits for Sarah. For a moment she had found a place where she could be free of fall-out from Laura's accident. She had escaped temporarily from her dreadful loss and was moving forward. Not for me. Laura's loss was under my skin like a tiny caterpillar gorging its way through a very large fruit. I wondered if there would ever be a time it would cocoon itself and be reduced to a painful abscess rather than a suppurating channel.

The undulating Northamptonshire countryside spread out before me, the river trailing through in a meandering graphite band. The footpath was muddy, the low fields close to the river flooded with the dark spillage of water. Crossing the weir, I spent some time leaning over the rail and watched. The water slewed over the concrete, brown blades chopping the icy water into cream froth. The path of the water seemed to change yet remained the same, the passage of water in perpetual motion.

From the river the ground gradually rose. The track way lifted from the flooded pasture and became drier under foot. I could see the top of Fotheringhay church, its octagonal tower distinctive. It dominated the landscape with its cathedral-like presence but I knew it was a deception. It had the illusion of grandeur. Only once you got quite close did you realise the trickery of its architecture. Near the church it became apparent that the nave had been halved leaving a stub remaining. It was still impressive with its flying buttresses formed from the warm local stone. Once the village would have been notable with its grand castle, church and priory; but the castle had gone as had the priory buildings that had once spread out from the church to the banks of the Nene.

The landscape was a beautiful monochrome print consisting of so many varieties of grey I regretted I had not brought my camera.

Water lay in what would have been the castle moat, now just ditches and streams. Half-dead trees, the trunks hollow, bathed tortuous branches in the pools creating abstract reflections of their lifeless limbs. One pool was so still and the day's colours such that it was difficult to tell which vision of the world was real and which the image. I stood at the edge of the pool and wondered if the reflection I saw was more viable than the place where I stood watching the mirror of water. Some particle or debris landed on the surface and the image smashed into geometric shapes, shards of broken glass.

There is nothing left of the castle's bricks and mortar; just a large mound on the edge of the village. I climbed to the top, the narrow steps sticky with clay soil. I noticed the crisped fronds of dead thistles spread over the ground, some still with dried husks of the thistle flowers. They were said to have been introduced here by Mary Queen of Scots. In February the nobility of the emblem had faded.

I expected to recognise the presence of the passage of time, feel the resonance of lost souls imprisoned within. But I only felt the sting of the wind and the consciousness of my own isolation.

From the information board I tried to work out where Mary might have been held prisoner, where the great hall had been, the place of her death, but I couldn't visualize it even with the artist's picture.

Where were all the ghosts of the past then? Why wouldn't Mary and her deceased comrades be here? I could only surmise there was nothing remaining binding them to this remote rural location. The place where a once impressive castle had stood was now reduced to a grassy mound in a farmer's field. As each stone had been removed, each item of furniture or object taken; had the spirits of the people that had used them and loved them departed with them? And Mary's ghost could not be here without a vessel to contain it; I believed it could only survive with a repository. In her case it would be the staircase.

A falcon spiralled slowly above the church tower, its black cut-out shape unmistakable against the steel of the sky. The bird mirrored the static symbol of royalty that adorned the tower. The copper of the icon gleamed momentarily under a stray thread of sunlight. Then everything returned to grey.

From my viewpoint I could see the thatched roofs and stone buildings of the attractive village. Across the river the line of trees on the horizon started to blur and I could see the roll of cloud bringing rain. They swelled like contusions, mushrooming into bruises that mottled the sky with an indigo palette, bringing colour to the previously grey scene.

I descended the mound, distant thunder thickening the air with menace.

As I started back, the rain began to fall in a mist that softened the edges of the landscape into a dreamlike focus.

All was falling. Water drops, water over the weir and my footsteps continually pulled down to the ground. That was the essence of nature; the pull of the earth's forces willing everything to return to the earth. Ashes to ashes, dust to dust. And water forever rising and clouding and falling. Spilling, splashing, permeating all things, whether we noticed or not.

It was late afternoon when I returned to the town. The fine drizzle had continued. It was gentle, a soft teasing caress that had been quite refreshing when it had started but by the time I arrived on the outskirts of Oundle it had soaked me. My newly laundered jacket had reverted to a dark green heaviness and my hands remained moist when I pushed them into the deep pockets.

Feeling uncomfortable I decided to make my way directly home. Perhaps Ratty would have returned from whatever adventure she had been on. We would have tea together.

I was striding out, head down, my hair stuck against my forehead. I passed the school buildings and the playing fields opposite and came towards the cenotaph and the Talbot Hotel. If I had considered it, I should have avoided that route.

There seemed to be a crescendo of noise as I drew closer. Still I kept my head down and was about to turn the corner when I glimpsed the familiar colours of a police car parked just inside the yard entrance. It made me turn.

By the side door were several individuals, a couple of regulars and Mac, looking worried. The scene resembled a textured crayon sketch due to the slant of the rain. Two police officers were trying to get past the people to their car. They were holding boxes of some sort and saying words in raised voices. The rest of the group were all shouting as well but it was Mac's accent that carried above the melee.

"Na, ye can na take them. I need them. Please do na take them."

I wandered over wondering what was in the boxes.

One of the police officers turned to Mac, struggling with the weight of the object he was carrying.

"Sorry Sir we have a warrant. You've got the documentation, now please ask your friends to leave us to do our job."

I was near enough now to see that they weren't boxes but computers.

One of Mac's friends was pushing nearer to the officer's arm, as if he might pull it at any moment.

"He's done nothing wrong. Can't you leave him be?"

Mac, used to dealing with bar room brawls said with threatening calm, "Come away, John. There's nought we can do. Let them take them. Come away now."

The small man reluctantly pulled back looking as though he was ready for a fight. Over his head Mac saw me.

I felt caught in two battles at once. The first was the quarrel Mac was embroiled in, the second was the one in my head which said I did not want to speak to Mac and was urging me to run away. My legs weren't responding, as if I had been shell shocked.

Mac spoke directly at me, as if I had enquired about the activities outside the Hotel.

"Phil, I do na know what's going on. There's no' much I can do."

I wanted to leave but found I could not. I was beginning to shiver. Seeing my sodden state, he said, "Come in and get dry."

Just as the officers were fastening their seatbelts and were ready to pull away, Jamie came to the door.

"What the hell! Ye've not let them take my computer? Tell me you've not let them take anything?"

He thumped Mac's arm as he ran past. Putting his hands on the boot of the police car as it pulled carefully out of the yard, he shouted, "Stop, stop, Filth!"

John immediately jumped forward again, his fists clenched at the passenger window. The engine revved more loudly and the car sped away skidding slightly on the damp cobbles of the yard.

Jamie went straight over to his brother and gripped his upper arms.

"We don't need to fight," Mac said firmly.

"Fuck you!" spat Jamie, releasing his hold with such force that Mac's arms snapped backwards.

Jamie stormed off. John started to follow but thought better of it and slunk away in the other direction.

"What was all that about?" I asked, still in a dazed state.

"Ye'd better come in."

We didn't go through to the bar but to a small back room that served as an office. It was altered though. On the floor where the computer should have been was merely a richer shaded square of carpet signifying its absence.

Mac went out and returned with two cups of coffee and a blanket. I took the dripping jacket off and wrapped the cover around my shoulders. I held the hot cup in both hands grateful for the warmth from the china seeping into my palms.

"I dunno what's going on," Mac said a hand on his forehead, his head shaking. "They arrived earlier, wanting to speak to me, and could they search the premises, did I have a computer and so on. Then it was who has access to the computers, what were they used for, all that. I answered them truthfully, but they did na want to know. I dunno what they're looking for. I told them the accounts were in order, that I'd paid my tax, everything up to date. They did na listen. What could they be looking for?"

I suspected those computers would be heading over to Peterborough to sit side by side with Kelly's computer and my Kirlian device, partaking in an alternative police line up.

I was feeling warmer and more comfortable. I reminded myself that I didn't have many friends and I ought to try not to repel any more. Mac had invited me in and been hospitable. I owed him something, I supposed.

"When they took me in, they thought I'd been e-mailing that young girl Emma. They took in Kelly Johnson's machine. Perhaps they're searching loads of computers?"

"Yeh, but why the Hotel?"

"Could be that a name or the Hotel name came up on Kelly's computer? I don't know how these things can be traced but that's the only thing I can think of."

"But I did na know this Kelly girl or tha' Emma."

"What about Jamie?"

Mac opened his mouth to make a denial, but before he had spoken anything more than the 'n' he stopped and closed his mouth.

"So Jamie could be involved?"

"I suppose. No, he's not involved." He shook his head more vigorously as if he were convincing himself.

I sneezed and started to shake again, not entirely due to my damp state. "I'd better go. Get dry. If you need me I'll be home."

"Aye. Thanks mate."

I pulled my saturated jacket back on. I left Mac sitting in the office. A man who usually seemed too big for the room, now overwhelmed by the space around him.

Only as I was crossing the square back to the flat did I realise Mac had not mentioned Sarah or our brief meeting earlier this morning. That suited me.

The drizzle was firmer as I reached the yard, but it made no difference, I couldn't get any wetter.

As I opened the door the unfamiliar scent of cleanliness greeted me and I remembered with satisfaction that the flat was clean. Flinging the door open in a grand gesture I was suddenly a man proud of his accommodation. Sadly there was nobody to invite over.

Before I went in I had a quick look around the yard but there was no sign of Ratty. She was probably holed up somewhere warm and dry and would return in her own time.

As I changed out of my wet garments, hanging them neatly from chairs rather than throwing them on the floor, I questioned why the hell the police had taken the Hotel computers. There obviously had to be something that linked the Hotel to Kelly Johnson and Emma Sutton. What, I had no idea. I didn't know enough about computers, except I did not trust them.

Before I went to bed I had a last check for Ratty. I even went to the top of the steps in my bare feet and called Ratty quietly. The nearly full moon was smudged by the still moist air. Ratty usually didn't like the damp and I was surprised she didn't come to the lighted doorway.

I called again. I wasn't sure but I thought I heard a noise coming from the yard. As I moved down the steps, aware of my cold feet on the wet metal, I heard shouting outside the gates, youthful yelps and laughter that paid no respect to the quiet street. Then the revving of a motorbike sounded, and more laughter. I slowly reversed to the top of the stairs. I hadn't gone far when Morelli's nephew crept into the yard. He was accompanied by the young girl I had seen him with before and they proceeded to kiss passionately, pressing against the wall so they fused into one entity in the dim shadows. Finally I crept back indoors, leaving them to their romance, still wondering what had happened to Ratty.

Chapter 17

At precisely nine a.m. the following morning I was waiting outside Paddy's shop, listening to the church clock sounding the hour and with the Kirlian device papers in my hand. As the lock on the door was scraped back I pushed inside. If Paddy was curious about my impatience he didn't show it. He returned to his place behind the counter and eyed me with suspicion.

"I had a problem with the last one. I need all the equipment again. I can pay you this time," I added, hoping this information would help.

Paddy reached slowly for his glasses out of his top pocket and slid them onto his nose. He then perused the sheets of paper and nodded. I fidgeted, moving from foot to foot. I wanted him to get on with it. It made no difference; he moved like a contented snail. But gradually the small pile accumulated and with each piece increasing the spoils I was filled with excitement. My mission to find Laura had been interrupted over the last few days but now I was back on track.

Finally, Paddy handed back the sheets of paper with a satisfied nod and grunted the sum of money I owed. It seemed a lot, but I carefully handed over my cash and waited patiently for the few pence change.

I was in business again.

I spent the rest of the day putting together the device and evaluating it. I had picked some leaves from any straggling evergreen bushes that I could find in neighbouring gardens to put it to the test. I created some 'aura' photos by placing a leaf on sheet film over the discharge plate. They were interesting but I was unable to reproduce the classic experiment. The one in which a leaf is cut in half but on the Kirlian photograph the silhouetted outline still shows an aura surrounding a whole leaf. Even so the photographs were beautiful, coloured spectrums that suggested paranormal spirits emanating from the internal unseen elements of each individual leaf.

By early evening my experimenting had lost some of its appeal and I needed a drink. I ambled down to the Talbot Hotel pretending I was not interested in what had happened yesterday afternoon.

Everything looked quite calm when I arrived; a couple of regulars at the bar, a few others drinking and chatting at the tables. Neither Mac nor Jamie was about. I exchanged a few words with the group at the bar, aware the reluctant conversation was reduced to monosyllables and so settled to sipping my well-deserved pint.

I was into my third glass and allowing the sweet heaviness start to weight my limbs when there was a clatter at the door. The police. D.I. Russell prowled in. He looked straight at me and fixed me with a mean stare. I didn't move. I expected him to come over and arrest me again, but he shifted his field of vision, looking about him. He made his way to the bar. Everybody in the room became hushed and observed him like a theatre audience.

"Where's Mr. MacDonald?" he demanded of the bar man.

"Would that be Mr. Paul MacDonald or Mr. Jamie MacDonald?" the barman answered, unshaken by the bullying question thrown at him.

"The one usually referred to as Mac."

"That would be Paul, then. He's in the office next to the reception desk."

I couldn't resist finding out a bit more, so I slipped off the bar stool and made for the gents, which I knew would take me out into the hotel foyer. I kept my distance from D.I Russell; I had no wish for his attention to return to me.

It was difficult to keep the pretence of going to the toilets and managing to hear what was said, but I heard voices being raised. I hid behind the door to the men's room, keeping it open to catch any drift of conversation. The name Emma Sutton filtered through to me and something about computer tests, then somebody flushed a toilet and it screened out any further tails of conversation.

Through the opening gap I could see people spilling out of the office room. Mac was being taken away by police officers, presumably under arrest. That scared me. People like Mac didn't get arrested, they talked things through sensibly and were believed. Not tonight.

I waited until I heard the slam of the police car door and then I crept out.

Looking up the staircase, I saw Jamie in a similar pose as if he had also been eavesdropping and had just crawled out to see if the coast was clear.

I was going to say something to him; I guessed he must have seen me. But by the time I reached the bottom of the stairs he had disappeared. He was probably too upset to talk about it.

I went back to the remains of my pint, but it had lost its interest. What the hell would Sarah do if Mac was arrested? And why arrest him anyway? They had wanted Mac. There must be a reason behind that. There seemed to be too many questions and not enough answers. I left the dregs of my beer and made my way back home.

I returned to the flat. Ratty was not there to welcome me but the machine was. The copper plate glittering and wonderful graced the kitchen table reflecting the magical light of the full moon. It made my spirits lift.

Chapter 18

I allowed myself to sleep late into the morning; I wanted to have as much energy as possible for the night's experiment. Going into the kitchen the machine welcomed me simply with its noble presence.

As I made a cup of coffee, I made the mistake of putting the radio on. My day was significant for the experiment I had to carry out. I had forgotten what people usually did on Valentine's Day. The radio was tuned into a Valentine's special request show.

Bunnikins requested a love song for Big Ears.

Why did people call themselves such odd things? I wondered if Bunnikins and Big Ears were aurally compromised and had at last found the perfect partner in one another. They could be anybody, just as likely the girl at the supermarket checkout and the delivery boy, or a merchant banker and his mistress. You didn't know. They could be anybody. You could hide behind a name.

A soppy tune about love filled the room. I thought of Mac and Sarah, or should I say Paul and Sarah. But he wasn't Paul to me. I couldn't have had a drink and a laugh with Paul. Like a polymorph the chemical make-up was the same but Sarah and I saw something different. Perhaps for Sarah it was easier to leave 'Mac' as my friend, perhaps that didn't seem so much of a betrayal.

In a way all of us were loaded with similar multiple personalities. When I had written political or weighty pieces for the paper I had always been Philip G. Lockley; for general use and work colleagues I'd be Philip and then to close friends and family Phil. There was even a brief episode at college when I'd flirted with 'Pip', which was probably a mistake.

And then in another life, a long time ago I had been called Daddy. All of a sudden it had become Dad. When I thought back I should have been able to pinpoint the exact moment it had occurred, but I could not. Those changes are metamorphic. You're never certain when the exact moment of alteration is, where one cycle begins and the other ends. Those two small letters signified such a huge change. I couldn't describe it but the loss of 'dy' had not meant I was different but that I had altered in the eyes of my daughter and it demarcated the boundary of the relationship between us which had changed irrevocably.

The Police song 'Every breath you take' came on the radio. Sarah had always said this was 'our song'. It had been the song we had first danced to. That had been over twenty years ago. The words initially suggest that every breath taken, or every movement made, is viewed by a loving observer. But on a different level they convey a more menacing message of an unhealthy, addictive lust.

I've always told Sarah that it's not a romantic love song. It's about obsessional love, always being followed, always being watched. She'd said it didn't matter and that she always thought of us when she heard it. Usually I could listen to the song without the floodgate of reminiscence opening, but now the memories overwhelmed me.

I could see an eighteen year old Sarah in her ball gown, dangerously revealing her pale shoulders. They had a luminous quality about them, giving the impression of newly exposed shoots. Her hair was pulled up and revealed her slender neck. Stray tendrils of hair escaped from her hair band and coiled and turned in glossy strands under the glitter ball light, gleaming like glamorous, adorning feathers.

I shouldn't really have been dancing at all. I was there to report on the 'Young Farmer's ball 1983'. In the national press, there had been a few very negative articles about the antics of some Young Farmers and I had been sent to cover this local event. My boss, I suspected, wanted some dirty story about the debauchery of youth and being the youngest on the team had sent me as some kind of undercover agent. Looking about I presumed that tonight's party-goers had been instructed to be on their best behaviour. More usually the type of entertainment I had access to was the pub, where rock bands created loud noise in the back rooms. We'd move frantically to the beat fuelled by beer. It could not be considered dancing. Our evenings followed a similar pattern. We'd shout at each other across smoke filled rooms, calling it conversation. We'd drink too much, chain smoke and eat a curry on the way home and throw up. There was no posturing to convention. That night I was an impostor. Dressed up in a badly fitting dinner jacket and a pair of shoes that pinched, I had driven out to a barn where the ball was held. Not a dilapidated metal construction with an earth floor, but a stone-built building with a concrete floor located within the vast acreage of a manor farm estate.

Everybody was quite friendly but not particularly interested in the man from the paper. I had not noticed Sarah when I walked in. It was her older sister, Clare, who was hovering about greeting people. I went up and introduced myself, handing her one of the new business cards I had recently had printed.

"Oh, I'll get Sarah to deal with you," Clare said, as if I was a nuisance and about to be handed over to the most inept member of the team.

I could not say that it was love at first sight. My initial thought was what a wonderful subject for a photograph Sarah would make. There was a luminosity about her manner and complexion which with care could be captured on film and create an ideal portrait in the style of the old black and white movie stars. I thought, 'Girl with a light bulb', and was putting together the composition in my head. She'd had to raise her voice above the background noise to nudge me from the trance.

Sarah led me through the crowds and with efficiency had guided me towards the leaders of the group.

"I'll tell you the best people to talk to, Philip," she said. "You'll want to speak to the president and some of the committee members."

She had continued to introduce me to enough people, before they got drunk, for me to get the information I needed for my article. She was friendly to each person she met, either touching their arm or kissing their cheek. I expected she knew something important about each and would make them feel comfortable in any social situation. Did you learn this kind of skill or was it innate? I had relied on these social skills when we had first married, gone to parties and held dinners at home. We seemed to have so many friends then. Now my life was filled with acquaintances and strangers.

Sarah had been so vivacious the first evening we met, it was impossible to compare her to the woman she had become in the last two years. That evening she had been open and bright, now grief had twisted her into frazzled strands.

After chatting with some of the Young Farmers' committee members I looked up to locate Sarah. I could see her dancing with a young man. He was very tall so their dance looked odd, Sarah smiling up at him and his long arms curved around trying to gather her in an intimate clinch. It didn't work due to their height differential.

I packed up my notebook to leave. I was quite content to be going as I elbowed my way through the growing crowd and increasing noise and wondered whether I'd manage to get back to town in time for last orders.

Somebody gripped my arm. At first lightly and then more firmly as I shook it off.

"Don't go yet, Philip," Sarah panted, as though she'd been running. "We haven't finished all the presentations yet."

I could have said no. I could have made my excuses and rushed to get a proper pint, but Sarah looked at me, not pleading or insistent but there was something persuasive about her smile. "We have to have one dance, anyway."

Before I had a chance to tell her that dancing was something I did not do she had grabbed my hand and was pulling me back through the crowd towards the dance floor. Everyone had just finished bopping several inches apart to a Michael Jackson song. As if caught in a conspiracy the mood changed as soon as I stepped onto the dance floor. The music switched to 'Every Breath You Take', causing all the couples to immediately take the opportunity to cling together in an audible suction of energy.

I'm not much of a dancer and was tempted to walk away but Sarah's grip on my hand was surprisingly strong so I felt unable to pull against the tide.

At the beginning of the song we had been awkward and danced a foot apart with our elbows braced. Gradually we had swayed closer, by mutual consent, until I could feel the shape of her against my body. Her perfume was delicate and intriguing to me. She seemed almost fragile and as my arms enclosed her I had felt stronger.

The song finished.

We did not immediately release our hold on each other. I was enjoying the sensation of her smooth body encased in her silky dress, and I let my hands move slowly down her back as if memorising the curve. Seeing our embrace the tall lad strode back with a frown directed at me from his intimidating height. He firmly removed Sarah from me and they shuffled back into their odd clinch. I left her to her lanky boyfriend with no pang of jealously. I don't think I even said goodbye. I certainly did not consciously consider meeting up with her again.

I did think of her though. My concentration should have been better as I drove down the rough track back to the Peterborough road, but I looked at my hands on the steering wheel and imagined them running over Sarah's body. I moved them caressingly over the fabric of the wheel imagining her soft female skin. She was unlike most of the women I met. They were either unapproachable colleagues in work mode and sensible attire or the rock music hangers-on who attended the back room gigs with their heavy boots, torn jumpers and piercing through any attractive feature.

There was a sudden movement from the right. I swerved the car, my halt assisted by a large tree trunk that dented the wing of the car. In the uneven patch of light, thrown by the now single working headlight, a deer stared at me, her eyes gleaming golden points. She was momentarily static, made rigid with fright. I was just as immovably startled. Then the creature bolted.

I reversed the car, aware of a new rattle above the old noises. The meeting seemed significant. Whatever the meaning of that encounter with the deer, that was the image I carried with me from the evening. It had felt like a premonition.

It is curious that Sarah always remembers that first dance and first song as though she knew we would have a future. I wondered if the song still reminded her of us, now that there was no us, or whether she dismissed it. Perhaps she had replaced it with an 'Our Song' with Mac.

I clicked off the radio with force, trying to switch off all the memories that old tunes can resurrect.

Even after showering, my body continued to consciously perspire. No matter how much I tried to ignore the weighty anxiety of tonight's experiment it pulsed, a noticeable tumour in my head pressing some autonomic nerve into fight or flight mode.

The water had been tepid but my usually cool palms remained warm and moist. The renewed device sat on the table inert. It drew me like a magnet and finally my digits could no longer resist tinkering with it. I tried to adjust a contact, unable to leave it alone. With my fumbling fingers I managed to loosen one of the wires rather than improve the connection. My forehead became peppered with sweat droplets. Now I would have to fix it.

Consumed with this task I disregarded the first tapping on the door, its gentleness unable to disturb my concentration. The second time the tapping was more insistent, and I looked up surprised. I rarely had visitors.

I opened the door cautiously, remembering my last guests had been the police and aware that D.I.Russell was still pursuing his case. However, my visitor was even less expected.

Sarah.

"Sarah," I said with amazement, opening the door wider. Sarah never visited me.

"Philip, something terrible's happened."

She swayed on the doorstep pale and nauseous. My immediate thought was 'Laura. Something awful has happened to Laura.' It took me a moment to remember Laura was dead. I had lived through that terror. Nothing would be as terrible again, even my own death.

So why was Sarah here, looking so alarming? She was too distraught for it to be a visit to arrange our graveside vigil on the anniversary of Laura's death.

"Do you want to come in?" I was hesitant, knowing it was unlikely that Sarah would come into my hovel but I thought she needed to sit or would faint on my doorstep.

"Okay."

I moved back for her allowing her to make her way into the kitchen unimpeded. I followed through after her and pulled out a chair so she could sit away from the other furniture in a solitary little island of her own. I remained standing, hovering above her unsure what to do. She sat primly, her knees tucked in, elbows by her sides and her neat hands clasped together. Above her, the non-shaded light bulb became conspicuous and her pose emphasised her vulnerability so I felt like a tormentor about to interrogate her. 'Girl with a light bulb' struck the old memories that had been rekindled earlier. This image jarred with the lovely one I had sensed in the morning. I could not help but sigh.

"You've tidied up," she suddenly said, and I sensed her relax a little.

"What is it Sarah? You're worrying me."

She had to take several breaths before she got the words out and then she could only croak them.

"Paul's been arrested." Either a cloud covered the window and the daylight dimmed causing a greenish shadow to fall on her face or she felt sick.

"I know. I was there last night." Now I felt like a traitor. I should have let her know. I told her what I had seen.

"Why?" she asked,

"Something to do with that girl, Emma Sutton. But I don't know, I really don't know."

She started to sniff and rummaged in her handbag for a neat pack of tissues. It took several moments for the procedure, but finally she blew her nose. She got up, dropped the tissue in the bin and returned to her previous position.

"I'm sorry. I didn't know who else to talk to. What can I do? You've been through this haven't you?"

I pulled up the other kitchen chair and sat leaning towards her but still an arms length away.

"I saw them take the computers from the Hotel. There must have been something on them linking it to the girl. Possibly a chat room conversation, something like that. That's what I thought the police said before they arrested him. Something about his name on a computer. D.I. Russell particularly asked for Mac."

"I don't understand though. Why would his name be linked to Emma Sutton's computer? I don't think he goes on computer chat lines."

"Would he tell you things like that?" I wondered how deep their relationship went. How many confidences had they exchanged?

Sarah shook her head. "Possibly not."

It hadn't struck me previously but Mac was probably lonely. Just because he ran a pub and Hotel and people were coming and going didn't mean he didn't feel alone. Dragged down here because of Jamie, when he'd have preferred to have remained in Edinburgh, it was quite likely he'd keep in touch and network using the computer.

"Maybe it's a misunderstanding anyway. That's how it was when they arrested me. They had a bit of information that turned out to be misinformation."

"I hope so," she sighed.

A sudden horrible thought entered my head and although I tried not to entertain it, it refused to go away. What if Mac had been involved? The thought started to ferment. If he had had something to do with Emma Sutton, had he been involved with Laura?

"You don't think he could be involved, do you?" I asked, feeling treacherous but unable to stop myself.

"Of course not!" She answered a little too loudly and we were both aware that however much we liked and trusted him there was a speck of uncertainty, a tiny radioactive particle capable of destroying relationships.

"What should I do?" The shaky whisper had returned.

"You can't do anything. Just be there as soon as he contacts you." I wished I'd had somebody so concerned about me when I was incarcerated.

"What if he has done something? I couldn't..." The sniffing started again.

"Look you don't know what's going to happen. The most likely thing is that there's been a mistake, and that he's not guilty of anything. They'll release him soon. If there is anything to find out you'll have to decide what to do then. Try not to worry."

I wanted to reach out to her and comfort her. I wanted to hold her so that I could feel her body supporting me. We had not realised it at the worst times but we were better together. I forced myself to reach my hand out, stretching it forward as if reaching for someone on a cliff ledge. She could grab it if she wanted. My pale scrawny limb looked like an old blanched branch, the sinews and tendons knotted with age. A branch you may not want to trust your full weight on. It started to shake a little with the effort of unsupported extension.

Sarah kept looking down, but I was sure she was aware of my gesture. Then slowly her right hand uncurled a little and the palm opened allowing the fingers to reach out. They moved in slow motion as she extended her hand up to mine, the slim digits tendrils searching for a hold. Our palms pressed together but I didn't constrict the pale fingers by clutching them. We sat, palm pressed to palm. A synapse that allowed a silent emotional exchange.

After what seemed a very long time, she looked up at me and managed a small smile which made me feel as if the sun had broken through the clouds.

The afternoon light was fading when we parted. As I showed her out of the front door the sky seemed cloudless. The night would be cold, perhaps with a frost, but at least it would be dry. At the top of the steps Sarah turned to me.

"We should go to Laura's grave."

I nodded non-commitally; I had my own agenda today and I didn't want to explain. She had already asked me about the machine. She'd looked at the contacts prints I'd made earlier with polite interest as I'd explained the concept of capturing the spirit of something. I told her half-truths about the Kirlian photography device and that I was going to use it for photographic experiments. She hadn't needed to know any more, having enough to think about. If she'd suspected I was going to raise Laura's spirit, she did not reveal it.

She continued with the arrangements for our painful appointment.

"Not today though," she said. "Perhaps tomorrow?"

"Yes." That would be alright, I thought, relieved. "Tomorrow at midday?" I suggested, knowing that my experiment would be over by then, and I would be able to concentrate on mourning Laura. Perhaps, if the experiment was successful, I would truly be able to lay her to rest. "I'll meet you there."

"Okay."

"Let me know what's happening with Mac."

I was going to add I was here if she needed me, but she knew that. I had already been able to prove it. A thought which made me feel less of a failure.

Chapter 19

I paced the flat, waiting. Watching for the night to arrive. I kept looking out of the window to see any hint of dusk edging on to the horizon. Once or twice I flicked the radio on, but the music seemed dour, the voices irksome. I paced some more. Then I sat. I went back and checked the case with trembling fingers, clicked the catches shut and then minutes later went back to recheck it, repack it and shut it. Then I sat again. Then I got up and checked the case.

The dark came with stealth. One minute there was dusk and then it was black, the transitional phase imperceptible. Even when the night came I had a long time to wait.

The window frames rattled intermittently, mirroring my vacillating unrest.

As I had thought, the sky was clear enough to see the pricking of stars and the shaved fullness of moon.

I was not scared of the dark. I had no fear of going into the night alone. The darkness did not trouble me as it might some people. I had spent too many nights comforting mother. She preferred subdued light as it did not hurt her eyes. I told her stories, trying to make her laugh. Occasionally I would be rewarded with a phlegmy chuckle and the outline of her white face smiling, as if she was happy that I had roused her from a deep sleep.

"Thanks for not abandoning me," she sometimes said, and would reach her frail fingers out to hold my hand.

There was a simplicity about night I could appreciate. In daylight you could see every blemish, each nuance of an object, every clash of colour, but at night it was all smoothed out and washed with a uniform grey.

I put extra clothing on under my jacket knowing it would be cold. Finally it was time to leave.

When I left the flat at about half past eleven, everywhere had an unusual hush so that my feet on the metal steps rang out, alerting everyone about my imminent actions. I felt like a thief, stealing away into the night.

People seemed to have vanished, the traffic non-existent. I was alone. There were dull street lights illuminating my path right down to the bypass, and then as I crossed the road into the fields I was engulfed in blackness. The moon shone brightly enough to guide me, without having to resort to the torch in my pocket. I didn't advance deep into the wood but remained on the path near to where it emerged on to the road.

After a few stands of trees it opened into a small glade. The must of leaf mould surrounded me, permeating the clearing with a deceptive warmth. The recently built, wooden plank bridge supported the new cycleway and path over the muddy ditch where I had stood what seemed like an age ago.

I turned the torch on, as the moon was now curtained by the structure of tree branches overhead. The torch light wavered but gave a pool of white so I could set up the device.

I took care. Unwound wires slowly, set the machine with great precision. Then I took the bottle of bark liquor and painted the wooden planks, posts and the trees trunks nearby. It seeped into the grooves of the graffiti heart and collected and spilled out. In the near darkness it coagulated into a sanguine dribble.

I was ready.

The hum of the trees and the percussion of their limbs with the irregular swell of the wind gave a macabre song to the night. The moon was on the wane, a stretched elliptical drum skin.

I hunched up on the ground, hugging my knees up to my chest within the circle of torchlight and pulled my jacket around me. The ground was damp. I could feel the fabric of my jeans cling coldly against my skin.

"One, two, three," I said out loud as though I was about to dive underwater. I switched off the torch and was swallowed up by the dark. It was momentary. Once my eyes had adjusted, the moon gave enough light to make out dull shapes. The familiar sturdiness of trunks against the frill of bushes, the curve of the bridge and upright posts.

Nothing happened. My buttocks became numb, my legs fixed, my fingers icy. It was freezing. I waited.

My breathing was audible. Regular pools of warmth issuing from me like comic book speech bubbles. Each one was filled with one word, 'Laura.' I willed her to appear. I strained every atom of my being to concentrate on her, reduced to each cell, each individual mitochondria, every strand of DNA. My body was aware of a reversal of inheritance in which every cell contained part of her. In the creation of her I had completed myself.

I must have smelt the change first. The musk of the damp wood faded and the air seemed fresh and cold. A hint of youthful perfume lingered about me.

Then I heard it.

It started with a faint drumming sound. The pulse of bicycle tyres over the plank cycle way. Pure joy. My tense body now thrilled with delight. I was going to see Laura.

But it was not.

The noise became pounding. Footsteps. Fast steps. Somebody running.

The apparition raced into the clearing. The image of a girl, made opaque by the vagaries of moon light. A kite of virtual fabric in the shape of a human being, trailed by an icy gust of wind.

She was screaming. I couldn't hear anything but the energy of the shrieking trapped me within it. I knew she was screaming. It stimulated the nerve endings of my whole body, so that every cell vibrated with the anguish of her terror. I covered my ears and crouched smaller, but the sensation of fear did not leave. I was pounded by its intensity. Shivering on the muddy ground I pressed my eye sockets into my knees.

The painting by Edward Munch filled my head. The screaming figure, unheard. Was I the observer or the observed? Was I the person bound by silent shrieking, whilst the world blurred and pooled around me. Was this how it felt to be insane?

When I looked up the figure had gone. It took some time for my eyes to refocus. In the moonlight, all appeared as it had before. But it was not.

The whole world had been stirred. What the hell did it mean? I had released something but it was not Laura. I clutched my head unable to think. I used the residual throbbing in my head as my excuse not to think.

But I knew what I had seen. I knew who I had seen.

Emma Sutton.

I retched, the sour sickness burning in my throat. My whole body trying to expel the truth of what I had just witnessed.

I hadn't found Laura.

I had exposed Emma Sutton, just before a terrible death.

She knew she was going to die. Just as Mary Queen of Scots had.

And where was Laura? Was she caught up in some equally horrific death masque?

Suddenly I was afraid. I was not only terrified of what I had seen, but also of what I had not seen, and could only imagine.

Emma had not been freed by the experiment, simply uncovered; the image would remain bound in this woody place, just as it would remain forever in my head.

I patted the ground to find the torch. It had rolled away. I couldn't find it and pushed forwards on to my knees, blindly scrabbling for it. My dead fingers finally grasped it and I managed to switch it on. The wavering light allowed shadows to play amidst the tree trunks. Calling. I heard them whooping. Or was it just the wind toying with my crazy mind? I could still hear the silent screaming. The air was raw with it, the wild branches clawing the night. I ran, feeling them tear against me. I had lost the path and was ripping through low scrub that caught and scratched me.

Then I found the road and sprinted back towards town.

I ran away, across the bridge into town, not really knowing where I was heading. Everywhere was deserted, no people, no cats, no nothing. Even my footsteps were noiseless. I was moving so quickly I don't think they even touched the ground. Perhaps I had been transformed into a ghost like state, or the Earth had disappeared beneath me. The only audible noise of my panic was my pounding heartbeat. It pulsated in my ears. I took it as a sign that I was still a physical being in the world and had not passed over to some alternate existence.

I arrived at Marti's door and beat on it feeling the smart on my knuckles. I was glad of a further proof that I was alive. Remarkably quickly the door creaked open revealing a slit of candlelight and Marti's eye spying through it. The eye blinked, taking in the mad man on the step.

"My god, Philip, What is it? You look…" She stopped. She might have been about to add 'awful' or 'desperate' but I think she was going to say, 'you look like you've seen a ghost', and had then thought better of it.

"You'd better come in."

I fell in and collapsed onto a chair, supporting my wilted body against the table. Tea appeared; it tasted so sweet it was thick on my tongue.

"Do you want to tell me about it?"

I was so drained and wretched I did not think I could speak.

"I guess you did the experiment?"

I nodded.

"You saw something?"

My lips felt numb. With difficulty I controlled my mouth to speak. "Yes," I wailed. "Yes, I saw something."

"Laura?"

I shook my head for a long time, letting it hang. "No. I saw Emma."

"Emma?"

"Yes. Emma Sutton."

"You met her. The girl that went missing. She's alive then?"

My head continued its perpetual shaking motion.

"I saw her ghost."

"What?"

"I saw her ghost!"

"You're sure?"

I wanted to scream at her. Why couldn't she just believe me? Would I have to tell her everything? Did I have to relive the horrible episode again?

She must have read my thoughts.

"Tell me in the morning. You're exhausted. You'd better stay here."

I leant my cheek down onto the cool grain of the table and closed my eyes. I wouldn't have had the energy to leave even if she'd wanted me to. I wanted to drift away somewhere peaceful without images or dreams.

"I'll never be able to sleep again," I told her, the words muffled by the sleeve of my jacket.

"I'll make you something, it'll help you sleep."

"Will it stop me dreaming, as well?"

Marti didn't answer the question but occupied herself with her task. It took her a few minutes before she placed a steaming concoction in front of me. The sleeping draught did not look particularly appealing. It was murky brown and smelt of cloves and lemon. The heat of the liquid was comforting and the taste bitter. It began to revive the feeling in my lips; at least it produced a response and drained away the sickness in my mouth.

Marti took my hand and I followed her up to the bedroom. I was not aware of the potion having any effect but my muscles felt heavy as we climbed the stairs. All my energy was sapped, so I let Marti undress me, and wipe my muddy hands and scratched face before tucking me into her bed. She got in beside me and rubbed my shoulders. I was telling her that I did not feel sleepy, just exhausted, but could not remember anything more until the morning.

Chapter 20

The comforting touch of human skin was with me when I awoke. My mind was at first oblivious to the events of last night. I caressed Marti awake and we made love under the cloudy weight of the duvet. It was only when I went to the bathroom to wash that the horrific images of the night before replayed. I looked at my gaunt reflection, elongated and wan, my cheeks criss-crossed with a network of scratches and remembered the screaming vision.

My reflection gazed back at me seemingly to respond on its own, with no initiation from my real features. I just replicated each movement. The droop of my head, wiping my forehead with my hand, smoothing my hair back. I had the uncanny sensation of being in a reversed world as if during last night I had stepped across a boundary and the reflection was now, in fact, the real world and I was just a virtual image moving due to the changing light. Ghost like. Steadily, I saw a bright aura develop around my opposite shape and my eyes felt heavy but could not look away.

My body became tense and I started to shake. I held onto the edge of the sink to steady myself. Minutes later Marti found me and returned me back to bed like a senile old man who has lost his way. I huddled under the covering unable to feel warm.

Marti brought me another drink, this one equally muddy in texture and revolting to taste.

She climbed in beside me and embraced me. Even the warmth of her failed to thaw the icy sensation within my bones. Miserably, I recognized that whatever had taken place some residue would always remain.

"Are you ready to talk?"

"What about the shop?" I asked, suddenly rational.

"Closed for the day. That's the advantage of being your own boss. Now are you ready to tell me?"

So I told her. Every terrible thing I could recall. Making my words vivid, so that she could not fail to believe me.

As I spoke her arms loosened around me, and she lolled her head closer against my shoulder, so my words were hushed by the curtain of her hair. She absorbed my story without speaking and then we sat in silence, cocooned by the duvet which contained our thoughts.

Slowly pricking through the fog of my ramblings another more insistent thought entered my head. "What time is it?"

"About twelve, I think," Marti said, turning to look up at a clock I could not see.

"Oh, my god! I was supposed to meet Sarah. I was supposed to meet Sarah at Laura's grave."

I was moving, throwing the cover back and trying to grab items of clothing. My layering of garments from the previous night made it difficult to assess what I needed and instead of things being tossed in their usual state, Marti had folded them over the chair. I picked a thing up and then dropped it, until it was an unfathomable heap.

"Philip. Calm down. You're not going to get anywhere like that." Marti came over and gradually found the garments necessary for a full set of clothes, and handed them to me in the relevant order.

"Go and see Sarah, and then come back."

"I've got to get the equipment from the wood," I said, wondering what a passer-by would make of the device. I didn't want to go back there on my own. "Will you come with me?"

Marti nodded. "Later. Now go and meet Sarah."

I left by the back door, and walked through the small side alley to where it joined the main street. Just as I turned I saw Sarah walking towards me. I did not know whether she had seen me, until she shouted.

"Philip?"

She hurried.

"Philip, there you are. I waited ten minutes but I didn't like waiting by myself. Shall we go down now?"

She looked around me, recognising the shop front, noticing the closed sign on the front door and realising the direction I had just come from.

"Oh." Her mouth remained slightly open and I imagined her thoughts running into some kind of picture of Marti and me; together.

"Oh," she repeated. "I'll go now. I've got to get back."

"Tomorrow! We'll go tomorrow." I called after her, but I wasn't sure she had heard me. Her back continued to move away with a tense hunch across her narrow shoulders. I felt terrible. I'd upset Sarah and missed going to Laura's grave on her anniversary. What a failure.

Leaning against the wall of the side alley I contemplated bricks again. Old stone bricks cobbled together with thick mortar. Hewn differently but similar to the prison wall. All stuck together, all dependant on the other bricks surrounding to make the wall firm. I kicked the bloody wall. It remained steadfast as it had done for over a hundred years, but I felt an oscillation start in my foot and continue as a satisfactory judder through my skeleton. I kicked it again.

Somebody was watching me. Turning I saw the Green Man plaque observing my behaviour. I was sure his carved eyebrows had just moved into a frown of disapproval.

My unscheduled meeting with Sarah had made me uncomfortable. I no longer wanted to return to Marti. It would have seemed disloyal.

There was still no sign of Ratty near the flat. I wandered down to the café below where Mr. Morelli was moving sacks of vegetables in the kitchen. He was a short man, his rotund figure a similar shape to the sacks and wasn't much taller than them. He was having difficulty pushing them about and his breathing was heavy.

"Have you seen the cat?" I asked from the doorway.

Morelli looked up, and tutted dramatically making it clear I was disturbing him.

"Wha' cat?"

"The little brown cat that hangs about the yard."

"Tha' bloody stray? I shoo it!"

Horrified, I stood gaping at him for a moment. I thought he meant he had shot poor Ratty, but he was making such exaggerated flapping motions with his hands I realised he had simply chased Ratty away.

Behind me I heard footsteps. Morelli called over me to the person approaching.

"Eh, Dean, 'ave you seen tha' bloody stray cat, Mr. Lock, he want to know?"

I didn't turn to see the nephew's face but could imagine his unhelpful grimace. So I was surprised to hear him reply pleasantly,

"Some of the kids were chasing it the other night," he said, as if this was quite a normal past time "Maybe it ran away?"

In front of me Morelli shrugged his square shoulders, so they reached to his ears, then he bent back to lift his sack making it clear our conversation was over.

I turned, finding it difficult to squeeze past Dean who was crowding the door way. I muttered a brief thanks and headed out of the yard. As I walked I searched about me for any signs of Ratty but there were none. Before I knew it I was crossing the bypass and into the fields heading towards Ashton Wood.

The ground was still hard with frost. The sun was a smashed star in the glassy grey expanse of sky. There was no warmth in it but it gave a sharp brightness that furnished the wood with crisp clean lines as if the dark pictures of the night had been erased and redrawn.

The nearer I got to the trees the less intimidated I felt. I didn't need Marti to hold my hand after all. This was a different place, transformed by the day. I stumbled towards the space where I had been last night. The warm fermentation of wood had returned; the whispering of the trees a friendly murmuring on the breeze. Even the police tape I had passed on the path had given up its urgent flapping and lay still.

The wooden slats of the path and bridge looked neat and unprepossessing. They simply were what they were supposed to be. An uncomplicated structure designed to cross a small stream.

The device was still there. It was coated with a fine mist of condensation so the metal plate was dulled. The suitcase's tartan cover looked forlorn. It was turned over and discarded at the edge of the glade. The bottle of developer had tipped over returning the remnants of the liquor to the leafy terrain, fanning into a black hand-shaped mark.

I collected the pieces together and placed them in the suitcase. I left the deserted spot; nothing more than my footprints and the stain of liquid remaining.

My heart was heavy as I trudged back to town, realising my search for Laura had come to a futile end. I had no idea what to do next. But as I reached my flat I considered that, in fact, my experiment hadn't been in vain. I had seen Emma. She was dead, had been murdered, I was sure of that. I couldn't do anything for Laura, but perhaps finding the truth about Emma would mean some reparation.

Chapter 21

I woke early, when the dawn was still muted. I was determined not to miss my meeting with Sarah. First I would hunt for Ratty. Though her comings and goings were sporadic, the place seemed forlorn in her absence. Her non-appearance left me with a sense of loss, a sense that another being I had become fond of had been wrenched away from me into the swirling current that seemed to seize everything. I couldn't let it be. I could not accept another loss. It would be like the picking of a scab so it would fester and never heal.

Resolved with my desire to find Ratty, I dressed hastily and went into the yard. I slung crates and damp cardboard about. Nothing. My movements were accompanied by Morelli's operatic tune which suffused the cold air from the warmth and light of the café. Due to the thumping and banging of things being moved in his back yard he finally came out.

"Wha' you do?" He flung his arms up like a musical conductor.

"I'm looking for my cat."

I don't think Morelli noticed that Ratty had suddenly become a possession, part of my family.

"Bloody cat," he said and went back inside.

I left the yard, walking slowly and observing any nook and cranny that might hold a frightened cat.

Further down the street, there was a tyre skid mark on the tarmac, and beyond it in the gutter a sinister stain, as though something had bled and been dragged. The liquid circulating within my own blood vessels felt as if it had congealed to the same consistency as the sticky smear on the tarmac. Laura. I thought of her crumpled, knocked-down body dragged along the road surface. I had to stop walking and take deep breaths or I would have thrown up. I closed my eyes and tried to think of nothingness, standing swaying in the street. Finally I regained enough momentum to move forward.

I followed the smear along the pavement, my stomach still sick at the thought of what I might find.

She was in the corner of a driveway. Hidden under the base of a hedge, her small brown shape half covered and camouflaged with decaying leaves.

I thought she was dead. The limp body weightless in my hands. One hind leg bloody and torn, the bone exposed. As I picked her up, with my fingers pressed around the bony ribcage, I felt a heart beat. At first I thought I might just be sensing my own pulse from within the pulp of my fingertips compressing the tiny frame. No. It was definitely a rhythm from inside the chest cavity. Ratty was alive. I wrapped her in the corner of my jacket and rushed home.

Removing the equipment from the suitcase, I padded it with an old t-shirt and constructed a sick bed for Ratty. Then I dripped milk into her mouth, much of it dribbling out. I attempted to clean the leg. Ratty did not open her eyes.

I needed help. I ripped the lid from the suitcase and carried the injured animal to the veterinary practice. They were helpful. Upset at seeing an animal in distress, they quickly assessed Ratty. I was pretty much ignored and Ratty was whisked away. I signed several forms and was told to come back tomorrow. It was made clear that they thought it unlikely she would survive. The odds were against it. If it had been a boxing match I would have backed the other side. I scuffed my way back up the street. Life was so bloody unfair.

The church clock started to chime the hour. With despair I realised it was twelve, and I was going to be late to meet Sarah, again.

I ran across the market square and down West Street towards the cemetery. When I arrived I slowed to a respectable pace and walked through the archway. Over the other side where Laura's grave was I could see the backs of two figures, one tall and masculine the other willowy and shorter. Mac and Sarah. I groaned inwardly, certain I did not want to share this moment with Mac.

I wandered over to them, still out of breath after running. They were standing so close their clothing touched but they weren't holding hands. They were not talking. Both of them turned quickly when I coughed to announce my arrival.

"You're out then," I said to Mac.

"Aye."

He didn't appear very happy about it. Without saying anything else he walked away, and then mooched about looking at various memorials, none of them having the slightest thing to do with him.

Sarah greeted me with a forced smile. "Should we say a prayer or something?"

I shrugged. I wished I had prepared a few words to make this an official anniversary occasion, or even brought some flowers. I had been too wrapped up in my own activities.

We stood silently over the grave, trying to connect to the buried being below.

The stone was a simple one with a carving of laurel leaves over her name, a small embellishment that signified nothing. She was gone. No matter how large the memorial or grandiose the carvings. No matter the length of prayers or brilliance of odes. She was gone.

Sarah's shoulders were shaking slightly; I thought she must be crying. The tears dribbling out unchecked. It was a silent spillage of anguish, unable to remain contained.

We stood like that for a time. Sarah was the first to move away. I heard her speaking quietly to Mac and I finally turned and walked over to them.

"I've got to get back to work," Sarah said her face still shiny with tears.

"I need a drink," Mac said mirroring my thoughts, "Ye coming?" He nodded the invitation at me, still without a smile.

The three of us walked up the road together. We stopped at the Talbot. Mac gave Sarah a demure kiss on the cheek, I presumed they restrained themselves for my benefit, and she continued on to the library. Mac and I went into the bar.

Tony, one of the regular bar staff, served us pints and we went to sit in one of the window seats, able to watch the busy room or look outside to small town life passing by. It seemed odd to be drinking with Mac without the bar counter between us. I was aware of a subtle change of position between us with the barrier removed, like meeting your dentist at a party out of uniform.

I watched a woman across the road waiting for her little dog to pee against a lamp post.

"What's going on Mac?"

He stared at his half pint as though seeking answers in the undisturbed foam. "Ye tell me. I don't know about your ghosts Philip but something terrible seems to have been stirred."

He looked about at the room full of contented strangers and said, "Let's move to the office. We can speak there."

I don't think I had ever seen Mac so distressed. Nor did I consider he would have chosen to confide in me unless something was seriously concerning him, something he couldn't discuss with Jamie. He sat hunched up and rubbed his hands together in agitation. He didn't look at me but watched his hands as if he were practising a complicated finger exercise. "Hell, Phil. I need to talk to someone."

He seemed to read my thoughts. This was extremely worrying. Nobody usually wanted or needed my advice. Yesterday Sarah had been to see me and now Mac wanted to talk to me. Unused to this position I said nothing and allowed Mac to continue.

"They found stuff on the computer. Messages between Mac and tha' Emma." He spoke about Mac as if it were somebody else. I shrunk back a little. Was he going to make excuses for his involvement?

"But it was na' me." He looked directly at me, his blue eyes flashing dangerously, so I would not dare to contradict him.

I wondered how he had got on with D.I. Russell's interrogation. I had pre-empted his thought pattern.

"Tha' detective thinks we got some kind a paedophile ring goin' on. I donna' know what to do."

He returned to his finger work.

"They let you go, though?"

"Aye, well I had to tell 'em in the end."

What had he had to tell them? My heart started beating faster. Was that why we were having this conversation away from the witnesses in the bar room? Was he some how altering his story to condemn me? Perhaps he had told them I was the ring leader. I expected to hear the thrill of sirens and D.I. Russell pounding on the door. I could feel the blood drain from my face and the warmth of it pooling in my ankles fixing me to the floor. This camaraderie was a sham after all.

"What have you said?" I finally asked.

He clasped his hands so tightly together I thought a knuckle might explode through the taut skin. "Jamie." He hissed, and began to hit his forehead on his fists.

So it wasn't me he was going to condemn. It was his own brother.

"Mac! Mac! For god's sake. Tell me what's happened."

He stood up so suddenly that again I pressed my self back in my chair uncertain of his next move, but he began to pace the room. His long legs taking him from one side to the other in three strides so his physical presence seemed to take over the space. It did appear to have some effect at calming him because after the first rapid steps they slowed to walking pace.

"I think tha' Jamie might be involved with this girl." He stopped for a moment, then continued to pace. "Nay, in fact I know Jamie had something to do with the girl. I should ha' said something before. A long time before."

His continual pacing had made me dizzy; I couldn't focus on what he had said.

"Jamie? Are you sure?"

"Maybe's I should ha' said something afore. Jamie's been in trouble before ye see. Well, you knew tha'. I think he used the name Mac on the computer."

"Did you tell that to the police?"

"I had to. Or they would have kept me in. They said they were gonna investigate. And now Jamie's gone. I don't know what to do."

"Was Jamie in trouble with young girls before then?" I questioned.

"Na. Not really. Or I'd ha' said something afore. I really would ha'." He looked at me with such pleading in his face that I finally understood. He thought Jamie had had something to do with Laura. I experienced a burning sensation in the centre of my being as if I was being slowly cooked from the inside. My innards appeared to stop their motion to concentrate on what Mac was saying. Was he was trying to apologise to me for not having let me know sooner?

Mac was so involved with his own dilemmas he did not seem to notice my stricken appearance.

"Back home he got involved with the wrong crowd. He was into drugs and the like and probably porn. He did ha' a young girlfriend, but I always thought she was legal age. There was some talk of girls from abroad. Ye know, a prostitute racket. Tha's when I decided we had to move. I thought Jamie had left it all behind too. You know how much he helps round here."

From somewhere my voice sounded. "So what makes you suspicious of him?"

"Well, he's a MacDonald too. It's just as likely for him to use the name Mac as me. He always liked to have a chat with the wee young girls too. At first I thought it was nothing, but looking back your Laura and that friend of hers used to come by sometimes, always askin' if Jamie was about. I thought it was them, young girls with a crush on him, but I didn't see him discouraging them. In fact, occasionally I found them in the cellars having a drag on a cigarette and giggling together. Like they were all young kids. Thing is I always think of Jamie as my wee brother, I always look out for him. I didn't think there could be anything wrong."

The words he was saying hit me in my inert stomach. One punch after the other. Jamie carrying on with my daughter, using her innocence for his own satisfaction. I remembered his comments about her being a lovely, bonnie lass. A bolus of hatred started to swell in my gut where the burning had begun. I could feel it slowly rising, tensing my arms. I would hit someone. I might hit Mac. At least it would be a kind of release. But I would wait. Mac was continuing.

"The thing is there might be nothing sinister about it anyways. He told me he liked that girl Emma, he wanted to go up to Edinburgh with her, show her the sights. Even the police said there was evidence of a train ticket being bought. So what's happened to her? Do you think Jamie has gone to meet her? Perhaps that's why he's disappeared."

"No," I said simply. Bits of puzzle locked into place. "Emma's dead."

"What? How do you know that?"

"I saw her ghost."

"Philip. What d'ya mean?" His hands rose to his head, the thick fingers combing through the short hair, in a gesture of bewilderment.

"I went to revive Laura's ghost, like I had with Mary Queen of Scots. I went on the anniversary of her death. Tuesday the fourteenth. I didn't see Laura's ghost, I saw Emma Sutton."

For the first time that evening Mac smiled. It wasn't a proper smile. His hands stopped their combing on his head. "Ye're mad, mate."

I thought he was going to get up and start pacing again as he rocked forward, but he stopped. "You're letting your imagination get the better of you." He didn't believe me. Just like he was denying his brother's crimes. How deep did brotherly love go? How far would Mac lie and cheat to keep his brother out of trouble, how much would he lie and cheat to himself that Jamie could not be involved? Jamie could tell Mac anything and he would be believed because they were brothers. I was telling Mac my truth and he was revoking it.

"Look, I'm only telling you what I saw. And what I saw was real to me. I think your brother killed Emma Sutton, and he may have harmed Laura." Now I stood up. I could not remain inert, I had been dormant for too long. I left, slamming the door but not knowing where to go. Not caring where I ended up, I made my way by automatic pilot back to my usual position at the bar. I drank a pint as quickly as I could. Thumping the empty glass back on the counter, I watched the froth sliding reluctantly down the sides and felt a little better. Tony refilled the glass, and I downed the second pint a little more slowly. I would drink myself into a stupor.

Gradually the beer anaesthetized my limbs, numbed the racing thoughts in my head. I slumped down on the stool.

Much later Mac appeared to take over the late shift. I grunted a goodnight to Tony. A couple of others used that as a cue to exit and Mac and I were alone, eyeing each other over the bar, not certain if we were friends or enemies.

Mac poured me a scotch and set it on the bar in front of me. I accepted it as an attempt at reconciliation. As I sipped it, the warmth reviving me, I was reminded of the evening two weeks ago when the concept of searching for ghosts had been set. Somehow the idea had seemed lighter then, not this heavy shadow that had stirred everything up infecting every aspect of my existence.

I was wondering whether it was time to leave when there was a draught from the door. It had been pushed open. I turned to look.

Jamie crept in. He looked rough as if he had spent days holed up somewhere uncomfortable. There was the haze of unshaven stubble on his chin and his clothes were creased. I sensed every hair on my body bristle like some crazed cartoon character, spiky with anger.

He ignored me but came over to the bar.

Mac looked relieved at Jamie's return. "Where ha' you been?"

Jamie didn't answer the question but asked his own, speaking in an urgent whisper to Mac.

"What did you tell the filth, brother? I haven't done nothing. Nothing."

"I didn't say anything. Look they got your records from Edinburgh. I just told them I hadn't been using my name to chat on the internet. The only way I could persuade them it wasn't me was to tell them the truth. It was you."

"Yeah, well tha' much may be true. But it means nothing."

"There's evidence tha' you arranged to meet the girl apparently."

"Yeah. Well we were goin' ta meet. But she never showed. Tha's the truth."

I didn't believe him. The rage in my body from before had burnt itself out and I felt remarkably calm.

"What about Laura?" I asked quietly and he jumped as if he had forgotten I was there.

"Wha' about her?"

"Did you arrange to meet her? Mac here tells me you used to have smoking sessions in the cellar."

"Well, the kid used to hang around. I liked her. Laura was a smart lassie. She wanted to go to Edinburgh with me. We were making arrangements."

"She was thirteen for god's sake. Didn't you think you ought to mention it to her parents?"

"No. She did na want you to know. You would ha' stopped her."

"You bet I would," I snarled.

The three of us were silent, each exchanging looks, not knowing what would be the next move, a game of poker where the whole pot depends on the turn of a single card.

I needed to know.

"Did you meet Laura in Ashton Wood, on Valentine's day?"

Through the aura of cool calm that surrounded me came a notion. It struck me like a hammer on thick ice. A romantic tryst on Valentine's day. Naively Laura had thought she would meet Jamie to organise her secret trip away with him. What had he done?

Jamie was looking at me uncertain as to what he should say.

"Look, she came of her own free will. She wanted to meet me."

"And?"

"It was Valentine's day. I kissed her, tha's all. She didn't like it, so I let her go."

I knew it hadn't been like that. I knew he would have pressed himself on her trying to devour her sweetness, the essence of youth. He would never tell me the truth. All I could do was create a nasty montage, cobbled together with my own experiences, things I had read about and heard. He had terrified her with his sudden physical advance and she had run. Perhaps he had pulled her, and she would have tried to fight him off, the helmet strap getting ripped. But he was big and lumbering; she was slight and moved too quickly for him amongst the trees. She had made it onto her bicycle. She must have thought she was free. Perhaps that was her final thought. I am free. In the next cruel movement she had been mowed down by the car coming along the road.

"Why didn't you stay around when she had the accident? Why didn't you help her?"

"There was nothing I could do. It was too late. Don't blame me, don't blame me." He lifted his hands up in a pathetic posture of surrender. He was tall and muscular. An adult. Of course he could have helped her.

And who else was there to blame? He was the one who had lured my precious daughter into the woods that evening and scared her into running blindly away into an oncoming car. My arm, as if weighted with its own mechanism, lifted, straightened and punched him squarely on the jaw.

He reeled back. Mac made a movement forwards.

Being unused to violence especially of my own initiation, I waited for a moment completely numbed by what I had just done, my brain taking time to adjust to the reflex response of my arm.

Jamie was obviously more practised in the art of fighting. He reacted quickly to my attack. I had hardly drawn a breath when his counter punch knocked me from the stool. I flailed my fists to keep him away but with little effect. Jamie's large hands were squeezing round my neck and I was having difficulty breathing.

Mac had come round to our side of the bar and was making noises, but neither of us paid any heed to him.

Jamie had been the reason that Laura was dead. I would kill him.

Unfortunately, I was not as strong and could feel Jamie's height and weight getting the better of me. My vision was blurring. I was going to lose consciousness.

Mac must have made some extra effort though and when I looked up from the floor I could see him struggling with Jamie, keeping his arms locked back and talking to him. I managed to crawl to my knees, feeling the swell of my face, the dribble of blood from my nose. My fingers had been bent backwards and felt strange. I could see Jamie's thunderous face, his eyes an explosion of blue steel.

"I'm going to ring the police," I panted, dragging myself up from the floor. Jamie was twisting and turning in Mac's grip and I was concerned that he might break free.

"Don't do tha', man," Jamie grunted. It was not a threat but more a plea.

"Nay, let's talk." That was Mac, for some reason trying to keep the peace. Still looking after his baby brother.

"No, not this time." I crawled away to the telephone in the office, hoping Mac would keep hold of Jamie. Any moment I expected the door to fly open and Jamie's fists to come battering down at me.

The call was confusing. My jaw was stiff and I could only mumble my request. At last the operator understood me and help was on its way.

It took a long time until I heard the distant sirens flaring through the night. Then the car door slamming and voices. The police sidled in, confronting me as if I were the perpetrator. I told them what I knew and two of them moved into the bar room. Immediately I heard raised voices. The other officer waited with me in the foyer. I realised why when moments later the entrance door opened again and D.I. Russell walked in. Even though it was very late and he must have been disturbed from his evening, he looked immaculate in his suit and clean shirt, his hair coiffed in its usual way. I wondered whether the man slept at all. Perhaps he was actually a robot that was switched off or on as needed, always ready for duty with no emotional input what so ever.

"You," he growled at me. "What's been happening?"

"Paul MacDonald's brother, Jamie, came in. He knows something about Laura's accident and probably about Emma too."

"You knock it out of him, did you?" He was looking at my bruised face, probably streaked with dried blood.

"He got the better of me."

The detective snorted and pushed past me into the bar. My chest felt doubly bruised even though his elbow had merely brushed my clothing. Russell turned briefly to say to the attendant officer, "Watch him," using his head to gesture towards me.

Through the glass doors I could see the police officers either side of Jamie. Mac had moved away and was sitting in my usual place at the corner of the bar. The whole scene was distorted through the small moulded glass panels so that everybody looked as if they had been trapped inside a hall of mirrors.

"Look, I ha' done nothing wrong," Jamie was shouting again.

Russell's reply was quieter and colder. He was asking questions. Why didn't they just take Jamie away? Arrest him and throw away the key? They kept questioning him for a long time. The detective with me, just stood and viewed the middle distance, like a dog sleeping with one eye opened in case I should make a move. We must have been waiting in silence for half an hour, when he suddenly looked around.

"Bloody hell it's cold." And he shivered visibly. He folded his arms across his chest to rub both arms.

I smiled, although my face hurt with the movement, thinking that Mary Queen of Scots might just be passing through.

D.I. Russell came back into the reception area; they didn't have Jamie with them. He remained in the bar. Free.

"Aren't you arresting him?" D.I. Russell gave me a withering stare. "He killed Laura!" I shouted trying to reach Russell and being forcibly restrained by the police officer.

D.I. Russell turned to me. "Mr. MacDonald has explained the situation to us. We know he was with Laura and he may be charged with leaving the scene of an accident. But your daughter's death was an accident, Mr. Lockley. I think we can say that much now."

"The computer chat though, surely that's illegal?"

"We found no evidence of any wrong doing in the computer interactions. The girls knew who he was, he didn't conceal his identity or age, nor was there unsuitable conversation." The detective sighed. "I don't know why I'm telling you all this, Mr. Lockley. But you're a journalist aren't you? Well, why don't you go and fabricate something for the local rag and stop pestering me!"

"What about Emma Sutton though. He killed Emma Sutton!"

"We have no evidence for that. As far as we know, Emma Sutton is not dead, just missing. Mr. MacDonald was arranging to meet her in Edinburgh, we believe she's there. We're making enquiries."

He moved away, preparing to leave. I ignored the pain in my upper body and pulled further forward from the arms clutching me. I had to stop him somehow. Make him realise the true extent of Jamie's involvement.

"But Emma's dead!"

The detective stopped mid step but did not turn. "What did you say, Mr. Lockley?"

"Emma Sutton is dead."

D.I. Russell turned slowly. He seemed to flow across the distance between us until he was very close to me, his grey eyes, ice cold, level with mine.

"And why would you think that, Mr. Lockley? When we all think she's in Edinburgh."

I wished his stare was not making me feel so cold. It seemed to be weakening me so I could only stutter, "I saw her ghost."

The glare suddenly melted and D.I. Russell's face was animated. He was rolling back on his heels and laughing. He slapped his legs. "Well, well, if Mr. Lockley here has seen Emma Sutton's ghost then she must be dead." He looked around involving his police companions in the joke. "That's how the police do things. Mr.Lockley has been ghost hunting again. We don't wait until we find a body. No, we accuse people of murder. We accept the opinion of mad people. I'm sorry for you Mr. Lockley, you must be crazy with grief at the loss of a child." He didn't sound sorry. "But don't drag us into your insane fantasies. Remember you can be arrested for wasting police time."

His face had returned to its position a few inches from mine. The irises hard steel. I remained very still; I knew he would like an excuse to march me away.

"Come on, Robbens, let him go now. This place gives me the creeps." I felt the police officer shove me as he let go, so I lurched forward, as if bowing in homage to the retreating detective inspector.

After they had left I stumbled wearily over to the stairs and sat on the bottom step, my head in my hands. Again I needed to consider my mental health. I was sure I was not mad, but how did you know? I expected most insane people believed they were acting entirely rationally; it was simply the boundaries of normality that had been stretched. And what did it matter in the end if I was sane or insane? Nobody believed me. People had to witness these things for themselves, even then they were likely to talk themselves out of it. And the worst truth was that before Laura's death I would have been on the side of the doubters, laughing along with D.I. Russell. Entertaining the belief of ghosts was the domain of mad men.

I didn't bother entering the bar. I could see the tall figures of the MacDonald brothers distort through the doors and didn't want to approach either of them.

I made my way back to the flat, across the cobbles of the market square. The air felt heavy as if the clouds were building in an ominous wall of water ready to break at any minute. The threat of the storm was a palpable entity and I was like an animal instinctively searching for shelter.

My body hurt. My bruised face hurt. My head hurt. The pressure of an approaching storm exerted an invisible pinch across the bridge of my damaged nose and my limbs felt restless as though my legs wanted to run but had forgotten how. My arms wanted to strike out but were too painful to lift and had nothing to hit against.

I went straight to my bed, with my bottle, and slept with my clothes on. It helped me feel less vulnerable.

Chapter 22

It was raining heavily the next day. The downpour was battering the building so it could not be ignored or slept through. Outside the whole world sounded as if it was disintegrating with the rain trying to reduce everything to rubble. I could hear the water flowing down the guttering, splattering and choking to the ground. It was the sound of earthly misery.

I fully expected the news about Ratty to be bad. Reluctant to hear the worst, I spent the morning pottering about achieving nothing, only an increased sense of dread. The rain continued all morning with an occasional distant roll of thunder ominous in the distance. I gave in. I cleaned myself up a bit, bandaged my sore fingers, and then made my way up the road to the vets.

The waiting room was busy when I arrived, various creatures peering from baskets and boxes. The human occupants gave me odd looks too, as if I was an exhibit at a topsy-turvy zoo. I felt claustrophobic. There was the musty smell of damp pets and their owners in the confined space. The windows were misted with condensation, giving the sensation of being stranded at sea.

The receptionist was busy with paperwork as I approached the desk. Finally she looked up. She looked at me blankly for a moment, taking in the black eye and bruised face. I wondered whether she was going to redirect me to the doctors' surgery. But then she smiled. "She's going to be fine." It took me a moment to realise what she meant.

"You mean Ratty's alright?" I felt the eavesdroppers behind me recoil.

"Yes," the girl said, "but now she's going to need a lot of TLC."

"Of course," I answered.

I was given a list of instructions and I listened intently to the orders. I didn't want anyone thinking the scruffy man with the beat-up face wasn't going to take this role seriously. Ratty was returned to me, still lifeless and with her eyes closed but with the leg neatly bandaged in pristine white. Even with the rain pouring down I felt a lot happier as I returned home, carrying Ratty in the half-case. We made quite a pair. Bruised and battered and each with a bandaged limb.

Ratty's small body was even more rat like when soaked with rain. If I was going to look after her properly, I would have to alter the rules of our friendship. I patted her body dry with a towel, the damp fur sticking up into spikes, reminiscent of modern hair styles. The hedgehog transformation did nothing for her. Momentarily she opened her eyes but they remained darkly unfocused.

"Ratty," I said, "You're home now," but the dim eyes closed. I didn't know whether she had any idea of where she was or that we were now officially flatmates.

I tucked her up and left her in the kitchen and went out to buy rations for us both. I determined not to be long.

As usual the supermarket was busy, the lights too bright, the piped musak too loud. I made my circuit as quickly as possible and hurried to the checkout. On the way past the news stand my eye glimpsed the head line of the local paper.

'Hunt for Emma…..'

I was holding the basket with my unbandaged hand and I had to put the basket down so I could manoeuvre the paper to read the other line of the title.

'Hunt for Emma moves to Edinburgh.' I took a copy and went to pay.

Back at the flat I perused the article. It appeared that the police were following leads. They suspected Emma had travelled to Edinburgh by train from Peterborough. The information in the article gave the impression that a ticket had been collected from the automatic machine. Anybody with any information or who might have seen her on the train should contact the police.

I knew she wasn't in Edinburgh. I knew she had never got on a train. She was dead. Murdered in Ashton Wood. I had seen her ghost. It was enough proof for me but the police wouldn't believe it until they had a body.

I looked over at Ratty, a small curve of brown fur in her improvised bed. She had been lost and I had found her. There was nothing else to do. I would have to find Emma's body. In some strange way I felt responsible. It was me who had resurrected her in her pain. She was like Laura, a thirteen year old caught up in the tangle of a complicated world which sometimes was impossible to understand. I had not seen Laura's ghost and I didn't have the inner strength to try again, so finding out the truth about Emma was the only option open to me.

I folded the slightly damp newspaper onto the table so I could see the headline. I concentrated on the print of Emma's name, hoping it would give me a clue. The body couldn't be in the wood or around the mill; the police had done a thorough search of the whole area. If Jamie had thrown it in the river she would have been found by now. Rivers had a way of giving up the dead. Everyone had been searching; there had been a couple of false alarms too. So where would Jamie hide a body?

I sat at the table, trying to put myself in that position. I had just killed somebody, probably not entirely meditated, but the girl was dead. What would I do? Panic? I thought of my reaction after the experiment. My first instinct had been to run. Run to somewhere I knew. Find a safe house.

Perhaps he wouldn't panic as much as me. He would have waited and planned things out. But I guessed he would still have taken the body somewhere familiar.

A startling thought came. If nobody believed me, if they had moved their hunt to Scotland, then it was up to me. I would have to find the body. I really didn't have a choice.

The only other person who knew Emma was dead was Jamie. I would have to talk to him. How I was going to approach him took me the rest of the afternoon to work out.

It was a long afternoon. The rain continued to beat down. The silvery sheet of water outside curtained the window and isolated us from the rest of the world. Ratty shifted in her bed occasionally, and her eyes flickered open blindly, but she did not fully waken.

Whilst sitting, my attention was caught by the now obsolete Kirlian device. It looked particularly forsaken. The once glossy copper was dull, the wires soiled after being left overnight and now I had roughly discarded it from the case to make a bed for Ratty.

It was a shame to abandon it. After all, it had worked. I knew it had worked even if nobody else believed me.

I did wonder why it had enabled me to see the ghost of Mary Queen of Scots and Emma Sutton. But not Laura. I may have been in the wrong place, of course. But there was something else. Something that had to do with the pain and pre-emptive suffering I had sensed.

In the early evening I decided to go to the Talbot and see if I could flush Jamie out. I needed him to know I was watching him.

Ratty had made little progress from her semi-conscious shuffling. I hoped she would not need me for a couple of hours. I mashed up some cat food with some milk and left the runny soup and a saucer of water for her in case she needed something to eat or drink.

I plodded my way across the square, still uncertain of my plan.

The streets were busy with the Friday night just starting, voices carrying across the street, happy greetings as people met up with each other. I continued my walk in a tunnel of concentration, a man on a mission.

I sidled into the bar and clambered onto my usual stool. Mac. Mac was on duty and I did not know what to say.

He finished fixing somebody a drink and moved over to me. "Pint?" he said.

I nodded.

"Look, sorry if……" I ran out of words. I was sorry and yet I wasn't sorry. His brother was a killer and he had failed to tell me or the police anything.

"It's aw'right, Phil. Not our argument. Have the drink on me."

And that was it. We had made our peace.

In this regained comradeship I asked, "How's Sarah?"

"She's fine. It's been tough for her this last week; what with the missing girl and Laura's anniversary, but you know tha'"

I did.

Mac moved round the bar to serve another customer and I enjoyed the taste and texture of my beer, sipping the sweet liquid through a perfect thickness of foam.

Looking up I could see Mac's back and was reminded of his brother. I remembered the reason I was here, and the liquid in my mouth that had been so mellow became rancid. Did I dare upset Mac, now we were friends again?

I toyed with my drink, but no longer wanted to taste it. I turned the pint round and round on the bar in front of me, observing the froth move across the surface and cling to the sides, and watched the reflections from the room pattern the sleeve of glass.

Mac remained busy, serving drinks and chatting to people. He seemed at home and confident, back to his performance as the perfect host. If he noticed that my pint wasn't being consumed or sensed I was unusually quiet, he made no mention of it and left me to my own thoughts. I wondered where Jamie was.

Each time Mac passed me, I nearly leaned forward and questioned him, but each time I hesitated and Mac had moved on to the next task before I had the chance.

It was late by the time I had plucked up the courage and the bar was emptying. I wondered whether I should get back to Ratty.

"Is Jamie about?" I asked, trying to appear unconcerned.

Mac almost jumped at the question as if I had said a dirty word. He started wiping the bar, with an urgent scrubbing.

"Nay. He's having the night off."

"I wanted to speak to him."

Mac stopped the wiping for a moment and looked directly at me. "I do na think tha' would be a good idea. Leave it be, Phil, for god's sake, leave it be."

He turned and began to wipe the other side of the bar but with less irritable motions.

I had to know. I sidled around the now deserted bar. Mac carried on his wiping, pretending not to notice me. I angled myself so he could not avoid seeing me and trying to keep my voice impassive said, "Mac, I really need to see Jamie. I'm not trying to make trouble."

Mac eyed me suspiciously, not really believing me.

"Wait then, I'll tell him you need to speak wi' him."

I watched him disappear, his figure reducing to a knotted blob as he departed beyond the glass door. He was gone for about five minutes.

I moved to a table by the fireplace. The flame of the fire was low. A log toppled as it was burnt away causing an effervescence of tiny gold embers. At least the glowing wood and coals gave off some warmth; I suddenly felt extremely cold.

Mac came back and shrugged at me his face inexpressive. "He'll be down."

I wondered which hotel room he was holed up in. I doubted he'd leave Emma Sutton's body there.

Jamie ambled in, arrogant and unsmiling, ten minutes later. Initially, he ignored me and strode behind the bar, pouring a scotch. Then he wandered over in a manner suggesting he had no option but to sit at my table. He moved a chair back churlishly and sat, his legs stretched out.

"Well!"

I didn't look at him; I kept staring at the glow of heat on a log, a transforming worm nibbling away leaving a trail of orange sparks. I was sitting close to the fire. I hoped it might outline me with a hint of red light, bestowing on me a physical menace which I was usually unable to obtain.

"I know that you killed Emma."

For a moment he said nothing, as if turned into stony silence by my question.

"Not this shit agin?" Jamie snorted.

He started to pull his legs back and rocked his body forward to move. As he began to stand he grabbed the half-empty glass of scotch. I moved more quickly. My hand reached out and grasped his wrist. A spray of scotch arced onto the table top leaving a trail of amber beads.

I looked at him then.

"I know you killed her," I hissed at him.

At first, he just shrugged, a defiant smile cruel on his lips. I stared him out.

"You know nothing. Fuck off!" and he pulled his wrist from my grip with more effort than he needed. He stamped away slamming the door.

My gaze returned to the fire, and I smiled. He hadn't denied it. An innocent man would have denied it. An innocent man would not have shrugged and smiled in an insolent way. He might still have cursed me, he may still have shouted at me, but he would have denied it. Jamie had not.

Without a thought I got up and made my way out into the hotel lobby, following him. I went to the base of the stairs and could hear heavy footsteps. Jamie had gone up. I would wait for him.

I sat at the bottom of the dark staircase. There was no moon; it had been washed out by the rain. The clock ticked. That was the only sound. The air was a cool still bubble around me, as if enclosing a moment in time. It was strange to be back sitting on these steps and felt quite different from the other occasions. I did not feel anxious or drunk but surrounded by a remarkable calm. I rummaged in my pocket, pulling out Laura's photo, but it was too dark to see anything but a blurred mass.

Laura, still remote and unreachable. Why hadn't I been able to see her ghost? Had the necessary reaction not occurred to capture a ghostly image of her last moments? Was that why I had not been able to see her? Or had the process of her death been different?

The dread of impending death Mary Queen of Scots had felt had been palpable, as had Emma's. A residual ache as if my nervous system had been shaken, passed through me at the memory. I shivered and hunched smaller on the stair.

Dread. Was that the same as pain? Another similar transfer of energy down bodily networks. Could those types of human energy be transferred, like the movement of light waves that were captured on film or X-rays? Impossible for the human eye to see but there none the less?

Perhaps Laura didn't know she was going to die. She had been traumatised but had made her escape. Her final energy was the certainty that she would live. It was different. It was an accident.

Mary and Emma had died with the fear and knowledge of their impending demise. That must be the key. The trauma of a terrifying death must give off an unknown energy with the capacity to bond with the surrounding environment leaving the ghostly residue.

The thought Laura might not have died in such anguish as I had witnessed from the other visions gave me comfort. I started to feel warmer. The continual ticking of the clock made me drowsy and I slept.

I awoke fixed like a crouched gargoyle, my mouth open, my tongue glued to the roof of my mouth with dried spittle. It was still dark although there was a promise of dawn edging the window in the stairwell above me. I was very cold. I rubbed my arms and tried to move, gradually stretching each limb out feeling the buzz of circulation press through the vessels. Finally I was able to lift my head and roll back my shoulders. As I stood up my frozen feet gave the sensation as if walking on pebbles. I paced around the lobby twice. The black clock hands stood out just enough against the old ivory face to indicate the time was five twenty-five.

My mouth was still dry, my tongue awkward. My stomach rumbled, unfolding from the cramped position but now acknowledging hunger. I walked some more, trying to regain control of my body. I was restricted due to the small space, and curbed due to the darkness.

I thought I heard a sound. The soft closure of a door from above. I pressed myself back against the wall hoping I should not stand out as a different tone of grey from the shadows around me.

A creak and footsteps descending the stairs.

I held my breath. Ghost or human?

Definitely human. I could hear the regular inhalation and exhalation of breath, whilst mine was held.

A tall charcoal figure lurched onto the black parchment of the lobby, and moved through. I could feel the movement of him by the eddy of air he had created. The hairs on my skin prickled. Jamie slipped outside, the door briefly letting in a subdued pre-dawn luminosity. I followed, keeping a few paces behind. I was still not aware of my breathing, as if I had been suspended in an animated state, a comic strip character moving across paper.

The smell of early morning was smog evaporating from the rain drenched ground. Cold and clinging. Jamie's large shaded shape moved around the back of the Hotel.

At the back of the Hotel were the car park and the entrance to the storage rooms and cellar. I could hear the rattle of the lock being opened and the swing of the metal door. Jamie's apparition disappeared, eaten by the black mouth of the doorway. I crept slowly after, dreading treading on anything that might give me away. Sidling through the door I listened. Jamie had descended the cellar steps. I had never been in here before but Jamie had tripped a light that gave me a moment to see the rough white-washed walls and steep stone staircase leading downwards. The light reduced its intensity and snapped off. Again I was in the gloom trying to remember where the edge of the steps had started.

There was no hand rail so I pressed my palm against the wall and started to go down. I slipped, grabbed out and caught hold of the step and managed to right myself before falling to the bottom of the stairs. My scrabbling must have made some noise and I expected Jamie's angry frame to appear at the bottom. I stayed where I was, a compromised insect, my fingers clinging to the step behind me in a painful reversed push up. I cursed my worn, damp trainers, one foot coming loose, the shoe lace dangling. A throb in my back suggested I had bruised my spine. In the moments of my awkward suspension, I was able to wonder, 'How have I ended up here? Hanging like a demented insect in a dark cellar.' I might be here because of Emma but her disappearance linked to Laura, which in turn connected to me and my search for her, no longer looking for her actual apparition but exposing the very formation of my being and her spirit within my psyche. I recognised that might be the essence of closure.

And so here I was, no longer searching for ghosts, but more tangible things. I was scared. I was also aware I was expendable. A maudlin air came over me and I wondered what would happen if Jamie found me. He could make me disappear down here. Nobody knew where I was. There was nobody to miss me. I could emerge as fragments of bone and dust in an archaeological investigation a hundred years from now. Or would I remain in ghostly form to haunt the cellars. Something touched my hand in the darkness. Not a ghost but some kind of scuttling thing. I resisted the urge to cry out and moved my hand slowly, trying to quell the shaking.

When Jamie's face didn't appear before me I continued my descent even more tentatively. At the bottom a glow of light ebbed from a lower room allowing me to make out brickwork and crates. Slowly I made my way along the narrow tunnel towards the light source. The underground spread out like a complicated task for a rat experiment. Short walls screening closet-like enclosures packed full of boxes and crates, which smelt of damp sawdust. The dull light allowed shadows to fall, creating mock barriers, making it more confusing. The sensation of my being a caged lab rat felt more acute, as if I had no choice in being here, nor in completing the puzzle. I paused, trying to get my bearings, aware I was underneath the bar rooms of the Talbot and that Jamie was somewhere ahead of me, I wasn't sure how far.

Then I heard him muttering. At first it was just grunts as if trying to move something heavy. Then it sounded as if he was conversing with somebody but there was no reply from the other participant. I crept towards the voices.

"Come on. Come on," Jamie was saying.

I edged round a corner of wall and saw Jamie at the end of the cellar room, trying to drag barrels.

"Come on. Come on."

He appeared to be wrestling with the barrel furthest away, rocking it into an open space. He moved suddenly across the room, and I flattened myself back against the wall. As I peered out again I could see he had fetched a trolley, and was heaving the barrel onto it. He continued his refrain of "Come on. Come on," until the object was finally set. He began to push it my way and again I moved quickly back. Too quickly, perhaps. Had he seen the shadow of my movement? He was certainly moving in my direction. Pushing back, I managed to hide myself behind a stack of crates in one of the closets off the main tunnel. I tried to stop breathing and vanish beneath the net of cobwebs I could feel around me. I heard his footsteps, his shuffling, his breathing. They came closer. The dusty hiding place made me want to choke. I stopped breathing again and closed my eyes, imagining myself invisible. In my uncomfortable position I was reminded of my night in the woods. I wondered whether chasing ghosts was actually preferable to pursuing real human beings.

All was quiet. He must have decided he was mistaken. "Bloody rats," I heard him mutter, as my toe pressed against a box I suspected must be rodent bait. Then I heard him moving again. A bumping sound as he dragged the trolley along. Coming past my hiding place. Through the criss-cross spaces between the tower of the crates, I saw the small wheels followed by his shoes, leaving a trail on the dusty floor.

More noise. Jamie irritated with himself and the barrel. I crept out and remaining on my hands and knees crawled along, following the marks in the dust to where he was. He had turned right at the bottom of the stairs into a different room. This area had a higher ceiling and a wooden trap door set in to it. Across the space was a crude pulley lift with a base platform and a rope. Jamie was trying to manhandle the barrel on to it.

It took some time; I was close enough to see the swell of the muscles in his arms and the look of determination on his face. Once the barrel was in place, Jamie took a hooked rod and undid the bolt under the trap door. The two panels flapped back revealing a still dark square of morning sky.

We were close to the cellar steps again, around the back of the Hotel. I supposed this must be an older, less used trap door down to the cellar rooms.

Once hooked up, the barrel was hoisted on the pulley and Jamie tied off the rope so that it was left dangling above the area of floor. I rolled back behind an inner wall as he strode across to grab the trolley and pull it behind him towards the exit. I heard him climb the steps and slam the outer door. Then there was a creak above me as the rope started to strain against the weight of the barrel and slowly swing upwards. Adjusting my crouched position I watched as the barrel swung away from the trap door up into Jamie's arms. The sound of the trolley on the gravel of the car park became fainter and I scrambled back up the stairs almost losing my footing again.

Pressing my back to the door I counted to twenty, taking a deep breath between each number. Only then did I turn and open the door a crack. I could not hear or see Jamie. I moved towards the trap door opening, looking about the car park for any movement. There was none.

A car engine sounded. Headlights flared on. I was caught, stranded in their beam. Jamie could not fail to see me. I remained rigid. The car door slammed and the ominous hard footsteps resounded like a count down.

Jamie faced me.

"You!" was all he said and he spat at me, the gob of spittle hitting me on the side of my nose. I was so frozen with fear I hardly felt it.

It happened in slow motion. The swing of his arm, the blanched tension of the fists, the pain vibrating through my skull. A simple thing.

It only took him a single punch to my jaw, and I fell. I was standing on the edge of the trap door. I flew backwards into space.

An intense pain radiated from my chin resonating in every fold and crevice of my brain, deep within my head. Then there was a moment of peaceful flight. He had killed me. I closed my eyes against the pink promise of dawn.

Chapter 23

Mary Queen of Scots was walking towards me from a far off distance. She was moving through a cloud-like tunnel; I blinked but could not see her clearly, only that she was surrounded by other figures. I could be watching a procession. Perhaps this was what it meant to have your whole life pass before you as you died. There were people closer to me as well. I could see faces and hear them talking quietly. I thought I recognised one. So if this was death, I was correct. My passing had been less traumatic than Laura's death had been. I had never really believed in an afterlife, but I may have been wrong about that. Heaven, I must definitely be in heaven because there was an angel smiling at me.

My limbs felt light as though I was being supported by a cushion. I was floating on a cloud into heaven. Perhaps Laura would be sent to greet me. I tried to crane my neck to look past the crowd, to see if I could see her and felt a prickling sensation in my back.

The muttering got closer and I felt a warm breath-like breeze near my ears. Somebody spoke my name.

The clouds continued to bob and scud across my vision. I heard a voice I recognised. A voice with the musical lilt of a Scottish accent. Mac.

"I think he's wakin'"

The haze began to lift, the clouds dispersing to the edge of my field of vision. Mary Queen of Scots diminished and became still, static like a picture. In fact moving my head a little I could see she was in a picture, the painting that hung on the wall in the Talbot Hotel.

Not dead then?

A stranger's face came towards me. Staring into mine, and pulling the skin below my eyes. "Philip. Can you hear me?" I felt warm fingertips push into the side of my neck.

The mouth made the same question again.

I groaned. The comfortable numbness that had seemed so pleasant had disappeared and I felt bruised as if I had been dropped from the sky. Expelled from paradise because of earthly misdemeanours. Heaven to earth in one easy movement.

My jaw felt especially jarred. It might never open again. My neck felt strange as if cupped by padded hands.

The face before me muttered encouraging words. "You're going to be alright Philip. Just stay still for now." Unable to tell them I doubted I would be able to move again, I simply made a guttural sound in an attempt at communication. It did nothing to relieve the pain.

Slowly the world revolved into focus. My eyes ached at the recognition of colour. Two fluorescent jackets identified the ambulance crew. Mac stood hovering and pale, his red head suddenly vibrant. From the window a silvery light kept flicking as if somebody was moving a mirror to the sun. The burning behind my eyes increased as the scene in front of me became clearer. There was a sticky sensation on my chin as though I had been dribbling glue. Later, I discovered blood had seeped from my lip where I had bitten it and I was dismayed to find it had soiled my recently washed jacket.

Chapter 24

They transported me to hospital. I had been strapped to a stretcher, a neck collar keeping my movements restricted. Mac came with me in the ambulance, a continual stream of apology issuing from him. I did not know why.

There was some amazement I hadn't done myself more harm. The consultant surmised I had been knocked unconscious before I hit the ground and had therefore been relaxed as I met the floor, just like a sleeper might do when falling out of bed.

A trail of people came to visit me. Sarah came in with Mac, looking wildly about her all the time as if attempting to spot any infections flying about. She stayed only briefly, hardly anytime passing between her applying antiseptic gel thoroughly to her hands on arrival and departure. I had never seen anyone else use the pump so diligently. They did, at least, stay long enough to tell me of Mac's heroic rescue.

He had woken early and gone to find Jamie, who was not in his room. He'd looked about for him and finally come round to the cellar, where he had found the trap doors open and a crumpled heap below. Me.

He'd picked me up and struggled with me into the bar room, laying me along a cushioned bench before phoning for an ambulance and the police. He apologised to me; according to the ambulance crew he shouldn't have moved me. He repeated he was sorry.

I forgave him. After all I had survived; as yet there was no indication of brain damage.

"It might be hard to tell," Mac made the standard joke.

I tried to smile but it was still too painful.

Marti came to see me, bringing a bottle of her special tonic. It looked and tasted remarkably like scotch. Her second gift was a crystal suspended by a blue ribbon. She hung it above the bed and said it would surround me with a positive healing energy. Finally, she kissed me on the lips, holding the pressure for a moment producing a thrill of pleasurable pain, as my lips were still swollen and bruised. I could remember the taste of her. I don't know which of her presents provided the most restorative power but after her visit I felt much better.

Detective Inspector Russell was also in the queue of attendees. He pulled up a chair and appeared so friendly I thought he might have brought me grapes. He had not. First impressions can be deceiving, and he was soon back to his normal pompous self.

He began by issuing a reprimand. "Mr.Lockley, we do not encourage members of the public becoming involved in the apprehension of violent criminals."

He did then relent a little saying that my intervention had helped close the case and he was relieved that I had not killed myself in the procedure. He boasted that the police had themselves been watching Jamie, as Jamie's previous police reports had given them cause for concern. That was part of the reason they had been able to capture him quickly after Mac had alerted them of my accident. The detective was obviously rather pleased with himself.

I didn't protest his moment of glory; I had no yearning to be the hero of the piece. D.I. Russell with his preening personality was much more desirous of that. At least Jamie had been arrested. When I had first arrived at the hospital I thought he might have escaped into thin air.

Mac had alerted the police as to the reason I might have been down in the cellars and the fact Jamie had taken the Hotel van. Jamie had been picked up by a squad car as he headed up the A1, presumably towards Edinburgh. In the back of the van they had made the grisly discovery of Emma Sutton's body in the barrel. Images of the poor compacted girl made my stomach turn, not only for her but her parents living through a nightmare just as Sarah and I had.

Jamie had made a full confession. He had strangled Emma. He refuted he had anything to do with Laura's death. Yes, he had met her in Ashton Wood but she had run from him.

Even Kelly and her mother came to see me. They did bring grapes. Kelly said nothing, remaining sulky faced and awkward whilst her mother talked about everything and nothing for half an hour, whilst she munched her way through her offering.

Chapter 25

Mac had said he'd collect me from the hospital, but I refused him. I treated myself to a taxi.

Beside the neck collar and half my face bruised to resemble purple chrysanthemums, I carried no other external marks of my accident. Under my skin every muscle and bone still ached. As long as I didn't laugh I would be fine.

The driver chattered on as we drove steadily back to Oundle. My head movement was limited due to the collar, so beside the odd monosyllabic reply I remained quiet, looking straight ahead at the grey road.

The market square seemed empty as the taxi drove around and I realised it was because the police unit had gone. The posters of Emma Sutton had also been removed, leaving only some flapping edges of the paper; a final resistance.

I had wanted to sneak into the flat unnoticed but as I was walking through the yard I heard Morelli shout something and come running out so I thought there might be a fire. He turned suddenly, raced back inside and then returned with a warm, foil-covered dish. Having been the villain to be ignored, I seemed to have become everybody's favourite charity.

The flat did not smell very pleasant when I walked in. My sprits sank. During the past two days my mind had been elsewhere and though understandable, I had completely forgotten about Ratty. Finally life had appeared to turn toward a more promising direction and now I expected to go into the kitchen and find the dead body of the little cat. My pessimism was unfounded. Ratty was alive. She politely stopped washing herself and meowed a greeting. Perhaps my life really was changing for the better.

Ratty had made a reciprocal recovery whilst I had been away. A little of the food had been eaten and the water dish empty. I refilled it and watched her limp out of her bed to reach it, having to hurdle over the edge of the case.

Whilst she drank I cleared out the soiled corner she had used as a toilet and regretted not organising a litter tray.

I opened all the windows and ignored the drizzle being thrown in with the wind. It was refreshing.

I was glad to be back. With Ratty to welcome me the place seemed like home. I went over to Ratty's box and stroked her. She produced what I considered to be a purr. It was not a regular purr like the throb of a motorbike engine, but rather an unpractised burping. Still, I accepted it in the manner of friendship it had been given.

Now I had cleaned up I could appreciate the delicious aroma of the dish that had been given to me and my taste buds started to pulse. It was time to feast. Even Ratty sniffed the air and looked at me hopefully. I pulled back the lid. Mr. Morelli's famous lasagne. Ratty and I would eat well today.

Before I even had time to lift the first succulent spoonful from the dish to a plate, there was a knock on the door. I nearly ignored it, the intensity of my appetite drawing me to the anticipation of lasagne. I needed the nourishment of food, not company, at present. Having enjoyed the attention given me in the hospital, I was now ready to be on my own again.

The rap came a little louder and I made my way to the door.

Sarah's face had a peachy glow which suggested she might have been embarrassed, but perhaps she climbed the steps quickly. The colour suited her. I had said nothing and was probably staring.

"I didn't think you ought to be on your own," was all she said.

With Sarah standing prettily in front of me my desire for solitude reduced.

"Come in," I said, as I sniffed the air. It was alright. The horrible stench from earlier had been reduced by the breeze blowing through. Relieved, I knew the room was tidy and the smell in the air was lasagne.

"I was just going to eat. Lasagne. Would you like some?"

She flinched, or I imagined she had. Perhaps I had been too forthright. I wondered whether she might suddenly panic and scarper to the street, but she didn't.

"Okay. Not much for me."

She stopped me as I scooped one spoonful of the meal on to her plate. I gladly served plenty on to mine and did not look at Ratty.

Sarah was very quiet whilst she nibbled her meal. We did not speak. She took tiny morsels from her fork and then seemed to have a thinking time before reaching for the next bit. I had finished my plateful well before she had finished hers, and I moved the fork around my plate awkwardly. The fork clattered disturbing the silence.

It was like being on a first date. We knew we liked each other, we knew we had a lot to say but initially could not find the right door to push through.

Finally Sarah put her fork down and said, "Delicious." Her plate didn't look entirely scraped and finished like mine. In other circumstances I might have put the plate down for Ratty, but did not want to give Sarah any reason to leave. So I ignored Ratty's little piquant face, peering over the edge of her case.

We both started to talk at the same time. I was going to say something witty about not making the lasagne myself, but let Sarah continue her sentence.

"Mac's going back to Edinburgh."

"Is he?" I wanted to say more to give me time to think but my head suddenly felt like a vacuum, preparing to echo with the words I thought she would say next. She was going to move to Edinburgh with Mac. Was that what she had come to tell me?

"You're going too?" I blurted out.

She stared at me for a moment and I thought she was trying to find the words to break it to me gently. The bruising of my body that for a while I had been unaware of suddenly started to throb again. My damaged face seemed to blossom and prickle.

Then she laughed. "No! What makes you think that?"

Because you've been seeing him, eating with him, sleeping with him. Fucking him! I wanted to shout coarsely, but I restrained myself.

"Because you've been having a relationship with him," I mumbled.

"A relationship?" Her forehead wrinkled and eyes narrowed in puzzlement.

"You mean *a relationship?*" she emphasised, her skin stretching and eyes widening, realising my meaning.

She shook her head. "Not like that. Mac's been a really good friend to me over the past months. He's helped me work things out, talk things through." My face must have retained a look of disbelief because she continued to explain herself. "When the police came to do their search, I nearly panicked, but Mac came over as soon as I called, even though it was really early. He really has been good to me."

She paused for some time, as if recalling all the helpful things Mac had done. I hoped she wasn't going to tell me about all of them in the same wistful tone. Then she looked directly at me and her face creased into a smile, I thought she was going to laugh at me again. "I can't believe you thought me and him were….well you know?"

She hadn't been standing where I'd been. However, looking at her barely touched food and her awkward posture, perched on the front of the chair as if ready to take flight I realised she was still far from for those intimacies I had imagined. With Mac or anybody else.

I was relieved. God I was relieved, but a nasty little voice echoed in my brain. 'Marti, Marti, what are you going to tell her about Marti'.

Sarah must have been able to read my thoughts. Perhaps my head had been damaged in my accident and my thoughts were seeping out for all to see.

"What about you and Marti. Is it serious?" She wasn't laughing any more; she looked down and examined her hands as if they were suddenly very important.

"No," I said quickly, and because I didn't want to say any more about Marti I pulled the daisy photo of Laura, Sarah and me, out of my pocket.

"Do you remember this?"

Sarah looked at it for a long time without speaking as if she were simply absorbing the energy of the happiness it portrayed.

"Of course, I do," she eventually said, then she peered at me, her forehead creasing into a frown and she looked directly at me with concern. "Phil, have you sorted yourself out over Laura?"

I looked back at her with similar candour, glad I was able to speak the truth to her.

"Yes. You see I know now that Laura didn't suffer. I know it was an accident. I can let her rest now."

I'm not entirely sure Sarah trusted my answer, but she didn't ask me more.

"Look I've got to be going," she said, "but I'll drop by again to check up on you." She said it with the tone of a librarian reminding me about overdue books.

"Thanks, I'll look forward to it," I told her truthfully, and then feeling like a boy on a first date blurted, "I could take you out sometime." It was both statement and question and said with the same desperation of that boy from the past.

Sarah was tactful as always and pretended not to notice my agitation, "That would be nice."

As she left I managed to kiss her cheek. Its softness, so delicate beneath my dry mouth, reminded me of new fruit. I caught the hint of her perfume as she moved her head away, so familiar yet with a different emphasis due to the passage of time; bruised flowers lingering forever on her skin.

Back in the kitchen I relented and let Ratty have her portion of lasagne, and then I sat at the table and picked up the daisy photograph. My experiment hadn't revealed Laura's ghost, but I felt as though I had found her. She was still here, a vital part of my composition, an integral bond between Sarah and I. Between the two of us we had created a family. Even with Laura gone perhaps we could still be a family. Her significance couldn't be erased, just as I couldn't delete her happy face from the photo in my hand; it was there with the persistence of chemistry.

With my stomach full and my thoughts more comfortable, ideas started to filter through. I would never forgive Jamie for his part in Laura's death, but I could live with the belief that she had not suffered before her death in the same way that Emma or even Mary Queen of Scots had.

I decided I was finished with ghost hunting. Writing and photography were my real skills. It was time to leave the ghosts to the past and move on.

I rummaged around for my old note book and pencil. There was a clean sheet amongst the forgotten scribbled-on pages which had been disregarded for two years and I started to write ideas down.

I could write about Mary Queen of Scots, her history or her execution.

Maybe I would see Marti later. Suggest writing an article on neo-paganism in the 21st Century. I would have to tell her that our relationship, such as it was, was over. It would difficult to tear myself away from the attraction she held for me. But there might be a chance for me and Sarah. I could not let that possibility slip away. Finally the fateful current had brought us close and I would have to renounce the warmth of the temporary harbour I had found. Marti might be upset, how much I could not calculate. Optimistically, I thought she might not be too unhappy if Sarah and I were to be reconciled. She might already have predicted it.

Still my meeting with Marti could wait until later. Something had flickered in my head and I scrabbled around for the AA flyer. It was rather crumpled and a crease ran across the dates but I was able to make out there was a meeting later that evening. If I got a move on I might just make the bus. This time I was ready to face the truth.